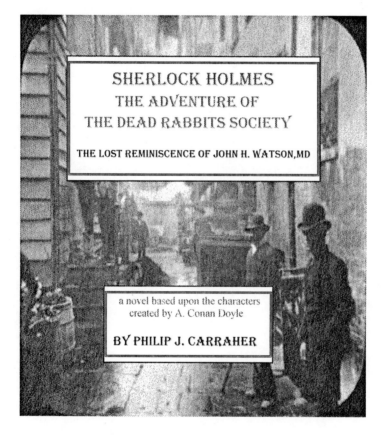

SHERLOCK HOLMES
THE ADVENTURE OF
THE DEAD RABBITS SOCIETY

THE LOST REMINISCENCE OF JOHN H. WATSON, MD

a novel based upon the characters
created by A. Conan Doyle

BY PHILIP J. CARRAHER

SHERLOCK HOLMES
THE ADVENTURE OF THE DEAD RABBITS SOCIETY

The Lost Reminiscence of John H. Watson, MD.

A novel based upon the characters created by A. Conan Doyle

by Philip J. Carraher

ISBN: 0-75960-513-0

This book is printed on acid free paper.

Title page photo: "Bandits' Roost" 1890 by Jacob A. Riis

1stBooks - rev. 9/28/01

Illustration by Sidney Paget, 1891,
for "The Red-headed League"

FOREWORD

It was with great disbelief that Cornelius J. Watson, a descendent of Doctor John H. Watson and his wife, Mary, nee Marsden, held the yellowed, dog-eared manuscript in his hands. In 1999, the pile of papers had been discovered lying at the bottom of an old steamer trunk which had come to belong to Cornelius by dint of his heritage. The trunk and its contents had lain forgotten and ignored in a corner of the basement of his family's house for as long as he was alive and no doubt so for many years prior to his birth. It was only a long overdue burst of curiosity as to its contents that brought him to it even now to dig to its bottom so long after his initial awareness of its presence.

The manuscript, subsequently authenticated and reproduced in full here, was never published. The reason for Doctor Watson's original hesitancy to allow the manuscript to see the light of day at the time of its being written, to instead store it away in his trunk, was not noted and remains unknown. It's discovery at this time is however cause for great elation among those who have followed the many cases of the great detective, Sherlock Holmes, as it not only presents an account of another of the detective's adventures but sheds some light upon those "missing" years during which Sherlock Holmes was presumed dead following his apparent demise at the Reichenbach Falls near Rosenlaui. While generally known that Holmes fled to "the Continent" at this time of his life, it was never before suspected that he'd made his way to New York City in America.

Here then is the lost "Adventure of the Dead Rabbits Society" as written by Doctor John H. Watson in 1908.

Philip J. Carraher, 2001.

INTRODUCTION

I have related to readers, in my reminiscence entitled "The Adventure of the Empty House" my profound shock and wonder at the sudden appearance before me of my friend and colleague whom I believed to my sorrow to be dead and departed from this veil of tears. A moment of "utter amazement" that caused me, for the first and last time in my life, to faint dead away and to, more happily, awake to the profound joy of resuming a friendship which I had thought to be gone forever.

Over the following years, my friend and I at times spoke of his reason for falsifying his death, i.e., the tremendous threat of Professor Moriarty's surviving criminal organization to Holmes' life and limb. Holmes quite literally was forced into hiding in order to secure his own continued existence. Initially, he sought refuge on the Continent but, following an attempt against his life in India that was very nearly successful and from which he considered himself lucky to have escaped intact, he thought it prudent to abandon Europe altogether. Immediately, he gained passage on a tramp steamer and made for America, to the burgeoning metropolis of New York City to be precise, and there resided in the relative safety he sought under the assumed name of Simon Hawkes. He remained in that city for a period of some months in the year of 1893, just prior to his return to London.

Of course, wherever he went, he found it impossible not to put to use those remarkable skills for which he has become, quite rightly, renowned. It was no different in the New World. Indeed, his skills were so much a part of him that it would have been impossible for him to do otherwise.

Readers of my previous reminisces relating to Holmes will be aware that the narrative that follows differs slightly in the writing from those preceding it, primarily due to the fact that I was not present nor participated in the events detailed within this particular history. The facts are coming to me second-hand, many of course from a most reliable source, Holmes himself.

Other events detailed here were however not related to me by my friend. When possible, I base those facts upon American newspaper accounts. In other instances, events simply had to be assumed, or rather deduced, for the sake of presenting to you, the reader, a cohesive narrative.

Holmes, as was the case with most of my writings regarding his work, was appalled by the finished product, roundly condemning the "romantic theatrics" contained therein when I presented the manuscript to him. He told me I'd produced more a dime novel than a scientific study of a criminal act and its resolution. I recall him still grumbling in his own unique way as he left me to return to his bees. I sincerely hope that you, dear reader, receive the following much more kindly than he.

John H. Watson, MD, 1908.

CHAPTER ONE

New life prodded her towards death.

Having climbed over the railing in the midst of the bridge's startling span, she stood gazing down at the water below, paralyzed for the moment by the enormity of what she was about to do, staring at the river's surface, only slightly brighter than the black of the night, with the look of one badly in need of solving a puzzle to which no solution can be seen. Her pretty face was battered, her left cheek was swollen grotesquely and was now plum coloured, evidence of the damage she'd suffered when beaten. Below her, the river glowed with its soft and strangely inviting movement. Behind her she could hear the hiss and growl of the bridge's cable cars moving by, ladened with passengers who were unaware and unconcerned with the drama taking place within the darkness through which they passed.

Only the wind, a soft night breeze, heard her sobs. To her right, she saw the lights of New York City, glowing like embers arranged in amazingly neat lines within the large black hearth of deep night. If she could grab up a metaphysical poker, perhaps she could stir up those logs, bring the embers to a blaze and maybe burn the whole place down. A strange thought of destruction to pop into her head now. Especially now. There were stars over the mantle of the hearth; perhaps the poker could be used to knock them from their inky foundation, to loosen them out of the heavens to fall with her to oblivion.

As she stared at the river's surface, it seemed to move closer to her. It was not faraway at all, close in fact, just a step and a short drop away, and seemed to offer gentleness. A friend, holding out to her a promise of peace, of release from fear and pain.

She was young, just eighteen years old, and was holding within her youthful body her lover's conceived child. A child brought into existence by a cad and scoundrel of a lover who

1

abandoned her as soon after being told of her condition as the earthly limits of the physics of speed would permit him. His betrayal broke her young and trusting heart.

Her secret, now her torment, was kept under lock and key for another three months until at last she was forced by her expanding appearance to summon the courage to reveal her condition to her parents.

Her father's fiery condemnation startled her. "Whore! Slut! Jezebel!" His words hit against her heart like stones fired from a slingshot. But not only words were used to condemn her. Her father, in his rage, hit her more than once. She still felt the pain of his beating, pain assuaged only in part by the absinthe she'd purchased after fleeing from the warmth of her home and trading her father's anger for the terror of wandering the unforgiving streets. She had only a few dollars in her possession and, coming across a tavern near the river, she spent it all, every penny, on absinthe, seeking instinctively, for she'd never experienced the drug previously, the gauze of its effect. The left side of her face was little more than a swollen wound by then. Desolation remained in her eyes.

The absinthe was not enough, there remained no money to purchase more, and now following her soul's quest for release from her terrible sorrow, a seeker of peace, she made her way to the middle of the great bridge's span to search out the comfort of additional oblivion.

"Oh God...God...please forgive me!" she cried to the unmoving stars above and before her. Then, tears running down her damaged face, she took another step forward, stepped onto emptiness and silently allowed the darkness to embrace her. Moments later, there was a soft splash, unheard by the world, then the waters of the river closed over her and its currents flowed on as before.

CHAPTER TWO

I have no doubt that Sherlock Holmes, while living under the alias of Simon Hawkes in New York City, recalled fondly more than once the Diogenes Club back in London, the organization of which his brother, Mycroft Holmes, was one of the founders. Holmes and his brother shared many consanguine traits, an aversion to romantic entanglements and a general difficulty to form close friendships being prime examples. Both shared too a desire at times to withdraw into their own thoughts and contemplations, not through any antisocial need but rather to allow that amazing faculty each possessed, their unmatched ability to reason, an opportunity to do its work without interruption. For this, the Diogenes Society was a godsend, its rules strictly forbidding as they did any member taking notice of any other member. No conversation was permitted at all save in the one room put aside for talk, the Strangers' Room.

No such establishment existed in New York City. If it had, I'm certain Holmes would have found it. As Simon Hawkes he'd taken up residence in a room offered by a males-only establishment known as "The Dead Rabbits Society" taking his meals in its dining room and his leisure in its rather large and luxurious parlor, the "reading room". It was here Hawkes was sitting in a comfortable seat near the warmth of the hearth, lost in thought, when his contemplations were interrupted by a friendly-toned voice.

"Mr. Hawkes, mind if I sit here?" inquired the man, pointing to the vacant armchair near Holmes. It was George Hammond, a longtime member of the Dead Rabbits and a man apparently in possession of an overpowering determination to achieve an acquaintance, to some degree or another, with every other individual who might tread upon the floors of the club. He was as gregarious as Holmes, when not engaged in the solving of a crime, was reticent.

3

Philip J. Carraher

Hammond earned his livelihood through his legal practice, one consisting primarily of estate work, and continued to do so even following his marriage to the beautiful Amelia Vanderholdt. The wealth of her family, a portion of which was granted as a dowry, would have enabled him to leave that drudgery far behind him if he had chosen to do so.

The Dead Rabbits Society obtained its unusual name from American slang. "Dead" in this case being New York City jargon meaning "best" while "rabbit" was a man to be feared, a formidable opponent. Leave it to the Americans to twist the King's English in such a manner. The society was located in a rather large three-story townhouse on Prince Street, just off Broadway. Rooms were available for rent as residences on the second and third floors and it was in one of these rooms in which Simon Hawkes now resided. The first, the main floor, held the space common for use to all members. When a "rabbit" entered the club, he passed by a male greeter who offered a cordial welcome and then inserted a peg next to the man's name on a large board to the right of the reception desk. A glance at the board holding the pegs indicated the members then present.

The main room in which Hammond and Hawkes now sat was tastefully and lavishly furnished. Wainscoting encircled the room, a soft wood paneling which was light brown in colour. Two fireplaces, one each on opposite sides, granted the chamber warmth. Adjoining the reading room was a billiards and card room. Next to that was the dining room and a kitchen offering members the opportunity to obtain a mediocre but edible meal. I am certain too that my friend also missed greatly the wonderful efforts of our own Mrs. Hudson at the time of his self-imposed exile.

Hawkes nodded his head, hiding his displeasure at the intrusion. He'd met the man once before and knew him to be an incorrigible conversationalist. He had to flee from his presence in that first instance.

"Raining cats and dogs. I'm glad my wife cancelled her plans to visit her parents tonight. Best to stay inside."

4

"Yet you dared to leave shelter to come here," responded Hawkes.

"What? Yes, I suppose that does show a lack of sense," he replied with good humour. "I see you reading the story of the body discovered in the river," he added, glancing at the copy of the *Times* in Hawkes' possession. "Another jumper off our modern engineering marvel, the Brooklyn Bridge. A shame, I suppose."

Hawkes nodded his head as his discerning eyes surveyed the man. Hammond was clad in a finely tailored suit, gold cufflinks sparkled with the firelight. The man was the picture of prosperity. His fine boots contained damp and mud on the heels and soles. It had poured that morning, cleared up by noon, and now at night, as evidenced by the shoes, it was raining heavily once more. The lower portion of the man's pants, by the cuffs, was wet as well.

"You have your own carriage, do you not?" inquired Hawkes. "Is it out of order?"

Hammond seemed a bit taken aback by the question. "Yes, of course I have a carriage and no, it's in fine shape. Why do you ask?"

Hawkes only shook his head in response. "No reason. I was just curious."

"I wonder why she threw herself into the river," remarked Hammond, returning the focus of the conversation to the news story.

"Despair, no doubt. Poor thing. She had been in the water a few days it seems, before floating to the surface and being fished out. A tragedy. A terrible sight."

"You talk as though you saw her."

"I did. The police called me to the river, wanting some assistance in making the determination of whether or not foul play was involved. There was evidence of brutality, that's why they called me, but this was subsequently explained by the father's admission of having hit her. That was brutality too of course, but not the sort that would cause the police to take

5

action–" Hawkes paused thoughtfully before concluding. "It seemed most probable to be the unfortunate result of an affair of the heart–and investigation subsequently bore this out. The police determined she was some months with child. An affair ending in abandonment and suicide. A tragic but unfortunately too commonplace event."

"That's right. You're a Scotland Yard man, aren't you?" stated Hammond, repeating the fabrication Holmes had promulgated to explain his past. "I've heard others mention it. May I ask, what is it brings a Scotland Yard detective to America?"

Another fabrication was at the ready. "Have you heard of the London Murders by the Ripper?"

Hammond's eyes widened. "Yes, indeed, that was news even here. A few years back. Good Lord, do you mean to say you believe your English Ripper has come to New York? Is he killing here now?"

"No, you need not fear about that. But it is a theory of mine, as well as that of another detective, John Littlechild who was deeply involved in the Ripper case, that someone who may have vital information about the identity of the killer has fled to America. It's that man I seek here."

"Heavens, why would anyone having such knowledge want to keep it from the authorities? Why shield such a heinous beast?"

"It is a possibility that the actual killer is a man of wealth who has paid to retain the other's silence. There is evidence that the Ripper is not from the lower class."

"Good heavens, I hope you find this man. Are you close to apprehending him?"

Hawkes shook his head. "So far I must say it doesn't look very good. And it must be remembered that I am here only to follow a theory. A slim one at best. Even if our man is located, an interview may prove only that our small hypothesis is incorrect. In the meantime, I offer my services to your local police force when I can."

"The suicide. You said just now that there was no foul play, at least in the sense that would allow the police to act. What did you mean by that?"

Hawkes laid the paper aside and produced his long cherrywood pipe, an indication that he surrendered any hope of further meditation. "The poor girl was pregnant and abandoned. Abandoned by her lover and, worse, by her own father. Her family is not wealthy but neither does it exist in poverty, the father is a successful meat dealer on the east side of your city. He had the means available to him to have supported her through this ordeal. True she erred, sinned, but was it such a sin that it demanded this terrible punishment? Her father is stern and he beat her, he admits to such, and in beating her drove her to her death, but in the eyes of the law he did no wrong. In fact, he is considered a man of high morals." Hawkes struck a match and lit his pipe. "I fail to agree with that judgement," he added as he sent a wreath of white smoke up to the ceiling. "To turn against his own blood at such a time, for such an ephemeral thing as honour—"

"Do the police know who the man, her lover, was?"

"No, there's no way to find him now," replied Hawkes.

"Well, she did shame her family, as well as herself," judged Hammond through a frown. "But I agree he, the father, was too severe. Our Lord asks us to forgive those who trespass. I am aware of a similar situation—"

Hammond was halted in mid-sentence by the sound of angry argument suddenly erupting in the subdued atmosphere of the room a short distance away. "So you've lost your tongue! You filthy black-hearted excuse for a man! You sniveling little runt! I've half a mind to beat you right now like the dog you are!" The speaker of these words of rage was Charles Dunmore, who had sprung up as he began shouting and now stood, his hands clenched threateningly, glaring down at the still seated object of his anger, his elder brother, Franklin Dunmore. Simon was acquainted in a cursory way with both men and knew the elder brother to be as ascetic and introverted as the other was

7

unrestrained and profligate. Simon understood that a public display of this sort, indeed any public display, was abhorrent to Franklin, a reserved and proper man. Even now the man was casting his eyes about the reading room, evidently more concerned over what others might think about the public spectacle than over the possibility of being physically beaten.

The two brothers were as opposite in their physical appearance as in their natures. Franklin being a thin stoop-shouldered man, only about five and a half feet in height, with black hair and a pale narrow face and his brother stocky and robust, a little less than six feet in height. His handsome face and flaxen hair made him a favourite of the ladies. Another opposite was added to the mix even now as Charles' face was red with rage, almost crimson, while all blood had drained from his brother's countenance, Franklin's black hair appearing even darker now against the chalky pallor of his skin.

Charles Dunmore was more than a little intoxicated, judged Simon, staring over at the two men.

Franklin placed a hand on his younger brother's arm, a gesture requesting he calm down and be seated, that he cease his public belligerence. Charles shook the hand off with a rough movement and, for a brief moment after, Franklin held his hand in the air as though unsure what to do with it. Finally he lowered it onto the arm of his chair. "Charlie, I don't understand you," he said in a low whisper, trying to keep his words out of the earshot of others. "But please lower your voice. If you feel you have a complaint against me we can discuss it rationally. There's no need to fly off the handle."

The younger man made an infuriated gesture. "Curse you Frank! Look at you! More concerned with propriety than about your brother's welfare!"

"Why are you shouting? Please–sit down."

"You go to hell! You go straight to hell!" With this outburst the young man abruptly turned his back on his brother and strode out of the room, the anger in his words reverberating in the hushed silence as he stormed away from his startled brother.

8

Franklin Dunmore stared at his brother's departing form with continued bewilderment until Charles was gone from sight. Then, to the surprise of almost everyone, he stood up and addressed the staring faces aimed in his direction.

"Gentlemen, on behalf of my brother, ah, and for myself as well–I apologize for this–ah, this display." He moved his hand to his mouth and coughed nervousness into the closed fist. "I'm sorry," he added and then he too walked from the room.

"That man has always been a bit of a prim prig," remarked Hammond after the elder Dunmore was gone.

"I wonder what they were arguing over. His brother seemed quite angry, whatever it was."

"Money most likely. Charles Dunmore is a womanizer and a gambler, continually in debt up to his eyes. He was probably trying to put the bite on his brother for some needed cash."

"A constant source of discontent. Money," remarked Hawkes. His thoughts briefly returned to the young woman who'd leapt to her death. Money, if she'd possessed it, would no doubt have kept her from suicide.

"It certainly is politically at this time. This country is being destroyed by the damned Sherman law. It's the cause of our recent economic depression. Thank God for President Cleveland. He correctly blames that legislation, the Sherman law, for the creation of too much money. He'll get the damned thing repealed. Get this country back on track. Keep us on the gold standard."

"I'm sorry, the Sherman law?" asked Hawkes.

"Oh, sorry, you're not aware of it, of course. I'm talking of the Sherman Silver Purchase Act passed a few years back, 1890 if memory serves me. It requires the U.S. treasury to purchase silver bullion each month, enormous amounts of silver. We're depleting our gold reserves to pay for it. Destroying our economy. Last May and June the stock market plunged. Some of our industries, even the railroads, are going bankrupt due to it."

"Hum, that may explain Dunmore's situation," said Hawkes casually, speaking to himself more than to Hammond.

"Explain what situation?"

"Did you notice the sleeve on Dunmore's jacket? An inch of seam has been sewn back together. A recent crude repair."

"Sleeve? No, I can't say I took notice of any sleeve. What does that have to do with anything?"

"Mr. Franklin Dunmore is a bachelor, living on his own?"

"That's right. He's never been married."

"Is he a scholar? Or does his profession involve much writing?"

"No, he lives off his investments. Has done so for years. Quite an impressive portfolio. I handled the writing of his will a few years back. That's how I come to know. You think he's taken a beating in the recent market downturn?"

"It's clear, is it not, that he's suffered a reversal of fortunes recently. Perhaps he denies his brother's request for money simply because he cannot afford it, or with the loss of much of his funds, is simply loath to lose more. It's equally clear that of late he's done much writing. Perhaps he's been forced to obtain employment of some kind, a clerk or a copyist, to make ends meet. One can't be certain of course without more data, but it is certainly a valid hypothesis for the moment, is it not?"

As Holmes related this moment to me years later back in London, I could not help but chuckle at the image I imagined, the picture in my mind of Mr. Hammond staring at Holmes with that same expression of befuddlement I myself have so often worn while in his company.

"Have you been talking to him? To Franklin?" asked Hammond. "Or with others about his situation?"

Hawkes, his face clouded in the midst of another release of tobacco smoke, replied, "Not at all. Except for a brief meeting with the man when I first arrived, I've never spoken to him. Nor to others about him. Why would I?"

"Come sir, you must have talked to someone. How else would you know these things, assuming they're true of course."

"I've already explained it to you. In part," returned Hawkes brusquely. "It is simply a matter of skilled observation and, with

10

the addition of a modicum of deduction and analysis, achieving through that observation specific enlightenment."

Hammond shook his head in perplexity. "I must seem ignorant to you, but I must say I remain seated here with still absolutely no idea of what you're talking about."

Hawkes sighed, relenting. "Forgive me, I at times forget that what is second-nature and obvious to me is not so to others. It is possible for a man who has trained himself in skills of observation, a man who knows what to look for, to glean from a person's appearance much information, even at times the person's history. Seeing Franklin Dunmore, I see at once a man who shuns physical activity and daylight. That is clear from his lack of colour and his own frail body. His attire, while of good quality, is generally untidy, suggesting the absence of a woman in his life. He is a man who is either ill or has had much to worry about of late, the lines of care and the dark shadows beneath the eyes attest to this. Given the other data, I would suppose it more probable that it is worry over his financial condition. He is a man who cannot afford to pay for a servant or a seamstress to mend his clothes but must now do such work himself. The fact that the repair on his coat, the seam just sewn together, lacks any quality, speaks to his doing the job himself. No seamstress could expect to do as poorly and get paid for it. This suggests a change of fortune. There is too the slight fraying of the cuffs of his jacket. He should replace it but has not. Even a man of frugality would have done so by now. But frugality can also be dismissed as the coat, while worn now, is of expensive quality, as is his linen and his jewelry. You saw the gold cufflinks and watch chain? No, it is not frugality that keeps Mr. Dunmore from purchasing new clothes but something else. The shine on his right sleeve, as well as a patch of wear on the elbow of his left, reveal he has spent many hours at a desk, writing. Since you tell me he has not done so previously, then we see again a sign of a change in fortune. Of course it is possible that he has suddenly decided to increase the amount of his correspondence or take up novel writing, but, given the other data I think it much more likely that he's been forced to supplement his income through employment of some kind. I fear he has suffered a reversal of fortune of late. Your mention of the Sherman Silver Purchase Act and its effects on the economic condition of your country and its people offers a possible explanation for this reversal, although of course that is pure speculation."

Hammond stared at Hawkes, clearly impressed. "My word, you read him like an open book. That is all–extremely clever, sir. Marvellous indeed."

"A trifle. Elementary," responded Hawks casually, smiling at the compliment.

A shadow of doubt descended over Hammond's sunny expression of admiration. "Of course, that's only if you're correct–" he murmured. "Meaning no disrespect."

"Of course," replied Hawkes with a shrug, the smile slipping away. He leaned forward and with a tap of his pipe against the brick, let the ashes of his tobacco fall into the hearth. "Now, I've had a long day and am quite done-up. I'm going to turn in, " he stated as he put his pipe away. "A goodnight to you, sir," he added as his long lean form rose up out of the armchair.

Hawkes left the room, now eager to go to his sleeping quarters and retrieve the morocco case containing his hypodermic syringe, desirous now of the morbid comfort afforded by his seven-per-cent solution of cocaine. Behind him, George Hammond sank deeper into his chair, staring into space, his gaze already obscured behind a mist of deep contemplation.

CHAPTER THREE

One week later to the day. The morning was a pleasant one in a sunny autumnal way, but with the evening and the setting of the sun came a chill deep enough to erase all sense of pleasantness stemming from the previous hours of relative warmth. It was Franklin Dunmore's habit to enjoy, well after his supper and just prior to his going to his bed, an evening stroll that without deviation involved his walking a quadrilateral composed of city streets and of which his house was both the start and the finish. His nightly walk consisted of his strolling two avenues over, then three streets up and then back again across the avenues and down to his house. This was the only exercise he routinely offered his body. Tonight, as he stuck his head out of the front door of his townhouse and felt the cold against the skin of his face, he found it necessary to go back inside and retrieve his overcoat. It, at least, showed no signs of age as of yet.

The wind picked up, pushing before it sheets of discarded newspaper and other bits of street detritus. The leafy branches of the trees lining the streets, the leaves already changing colours, swayed in the wind and hissed with protests over their disturbance. A half-moon was up in the darkened sky. The street-lamps threw off feeble circles of light and the pavement and building facades were shadow-draped with shifting pools of murk, the adumbration thrown off by the trees. Lamplight glowed in many windows, wan behind the drawn curtains, within the homes Dunmore passed by. As always, he made his way to Broadway and here slowed his step to gaze at the windows of the stores and shops that lined the avenue. Occasionally, in the past, if an item caught his eye he would enter a store and make a purchase. Now of course that small indulgence was impossible.

Up three streets north on Broadway and he changed direction, turning right, beginning to walk the top of the rectangle which would bring him back towards his home. Here, off the avenue, the street was as dark as the Yew Alley of Baskerville Hall. There came out of the black night off to Dunmore's left a flutter of sound and the frail man's heart skipped a beat over the noise, so very near him. A drunkard suddenly came out of the shadows, reeling on unsteady legs, and bumped forcibly against his arm and shoulder, very nearly knocking him to the ground. "Good God man!" he cried out. "Watch where you're going."

"'Cuse me," muttered the inebriate and then, a wipe of his sleeve across his runny nose, he shambled on his way. Dunmore stood watching the man's back, feeling his stomach churning from the fright he'd just received, until, the drunkard a distance away, he turned and continued on his way to his home.

A filigree of clouds moved in to cover the half-moon. Dunmore was very near his own house when, passing a narrow alley that intersected with the street, he thought he glimpsed out of the corner of his eye a movement within its obscurity, a shadow shifting within shadow. Abruptly a vague threat seemed to be lurking there in the gloom and Dunmore nervously hastened his step, now anxious to return to the safety of his own home.

"My imagination," he told himself even as he quickened the pace of his strides. In this attempt at small comfort he was swiftly disappointed. A sound, sharp and distinct, unmistakably that of a man stepping swiftly and immediately behind him, came to his ears. Before he had a chance to react or cry out, a thong of leather passed before his frightened eyes and tightly encircled his neck.

Attempting to shout out, to scream his terror and yell for help, he discovered himself incapable of producing a sound. The leather thong squeezed tight around his neck prohibited it! His screams remained bottled up inside him. I can't breathe! Dear God! I'm being strangled! Help me! I'm being murdered! His fingers grappled against the leather strap impotently, ineffectually.

A black stain crawled onto the edge of his sight and began to sweep over his eyes, the stain pulsing to the beat of his own terrified heart. He crumpled to his knees very near to unconsciousness, with despair hovering somewhere within his encroaching insensibility, the despair of one realizing he is about to die and being helpless, absolutely helpless, to resist it.

But he was wrong. He was not about to die. Suddenly, blessedly, the terrible restriction about his throat was removed, the tightness gone, and he was suddenly able to breathe once more. Gasping, he drew air into his lungs with great deep breaths. Still on his knees, he found himself listening to the wind and to the throbbing of his own frightened heart. A thread of drool ran from the corner of his slack mouth to the ledge of his trembling chin.

Gaining strength, he struggled to his feet, his legs wobbling beneath him like those of the drunkard he'd passed minutes earlier, and, still fearful and thankful to be alive, a condition he'd taken for granted only moments ago, he continued home, his hand massaging the pain now residing in his damaged throat.

CHAPTER FOUR

It was three days following the first attack upon Franklin Dunmore's person that the man made his appearance in front of Simon Hawkes, requesting the detective's assistance.

The entrance to The Dead Rabbits Society was on Prince Street but one side of the building in which the society resided faced onto Lafayette and it was Lafayette Street that Hawkes gazed upon from out the window of his room. Morning had brought with it a misty drizzle of rain, a London-like drizzle, and umbrellas were raised up against it. Some pedestrians had their collars up for shelter from the morning chill as well. A steady stream of cabs and carriages moved in the street and peddlers stood by their carts, despite the rain, on the sides of the street displaying the multitude of their wares, the horses in front of the carts patiently ignoring the passing pedestrians. Ennui, the nemesis of a mind such as that possessed by Hawkes, had held him in its grip for days now, forcing him daily to his small doses of cocaine. His seven-per-cent solution. This was so until the previous night when a case of interest was presented to him, an incident of blackmail against a citizen of high regard. His mind was contemplating the facts of this new case, as they were presented to him the previous evening, when, to his surprise, there came a knock upon his door, a tentative rapping upon the wood.

"Enter," shouted Hawkes, turning away from the window. The knob was turned, the door slowly pushed open and there stood Franklin Dunmore, his eyes blinking nervously at Hawkes, appearing like a man who'd inadvertently entered the wrong room and was astonished to find himself in the spot in which he was now standing. His face was haggard and worn, more so than when last Hawkes had seen the man. His hat and clothes were damp with the mist. "I beg your pardon, Mr. Hawkes," he said, "for coming unannounced and so early–"

"Mr. Dunmore," greeted Hawkes, surprised to see the man. "Come in. Pray, tell me, what brings you to my door." His eyes immediately went to the strip of bruised tissue running across Dunmore's throat and which was visible above the man's collar. "Lord, man, what's happened to you?" he inquired with true concern. "Are you all right?"

"I'm–fine. Thank you," returned Dunmore, his voice scarcely more than a raised whisper. "Or at least as well as I could be–under the circumstances. Mr. Hawkes, I know you to be a detective, of the London Scotland Yard and I-I understand you to be quite capable. George, George Hammond, has only just recommended you. It's at his suggestion I'm here. I've come–ah, on a personal matter in the hope that I will be able to obtain your, ah, services, if you are available."

"I have just last night been requested to become involved in a problem which may require much of my time, Mr. Dunmore," replied Hawkes. "I am therefore regretfully not available–"

Dunmore's eyes expanded with the very words he next uttered, as though amazed to hear them falling from his own quivering lips. "Please, Mr. Hawkes, someone, someone is trying to kill me. I want you to find out who it is." In the next moment, a sob escaped him. "Please don't turn me away! Please help me. Please!"

Hawkes pushed a chair to him. "Sit and compose yourself. May I get you a drink, some brandy?" Dunmore shook his head and Hawkes went and sat on the edge of the still unmade bed. It was a moment before Dunmore was able to speak again.

"Yes, I'm better now. Sorry."

"Someone attacked you, two or three days ago. The state of that ugly bruise around your neck says as much. It's had time to change colour. What brings you around to me now so long after?"

"You–are correct. I was attacked three days ago, at night. I put it down to the actions of a thief, an attempt by a common brigand to rob me, but there has been another, a second attempt on my life."

17

Hawkes leaned forward, a gleam appearing in his eyes. "Mr. Dunmore, tell me exactly what has happened. There have been two attempts against your life. Tell me of both, beginning with the first. I know how emotionally upsetting these things can be but please keep to the facts. Be as precise as your memory allows you to be."

"Yes, of course," replied the rasping Dunmore, passing the tip of his tongue over his dry lips. "Yes, well, the first attack occurred during my nightly constitutional. It's my habit to go out for a short stroll each night before going to bed. This one night, three nights ago, I was attacked by a man stepping out of an alley. I heard a noise behind me and the next moment I was being strangled. It was–"

"Strangled? Garroted, with a strap?" asked Hawkes. "Your wound says as much."

"Ah, yes, a strap of some kind, leather I think. He passed it over my head. It-It was around my throat in an instant. Before I had a chance to react—"

"A belt, perhaps?"

"It could've been. I really don't know."

"Your walk. You said it was a nightly habit. Do you find yourself invariably walking the same streets or do you alternate the course each night?

"I-I'm a creature of habit, Mr. Hawkes. I walk the same streets each night."

"I see. Please continue."

"Ah, I-I was suddenly being choked. To death I thought at the time. He had me down on the ground and I imagined I was done for. However he–he suddenly released the pressure on the strap around my neck, and then was gone. Just like that he let me go and vanished."

"Did you struggle against him?"

"I did as best I could, of course. But I'm not physically strong. I was really quite helpless against him."

"You think him to be a robber. Did he take anything from you?"

"No. That's the strangest thing. He made no effort to rob me of my wallet, or my pocket watch and chain. No, he simply stopped in his attack and left."

"Hum, that is quite unusual. Did you report the matter to the police?"

"Yes. They seemed to believe it was a thief. Although they could offer no explanation as to why a thief would attack and then leave without taking anything."

"Did you see your attacker at all?"

"No, I saw nothing. As I said, he struck from behind."

"Perhaps a glance at his shoes, or his pants?"

"Why yes, yes, now that you ask. I did see his shoes. They were well made. Of some quality now that I think of it."

"That is suggestive. Our thief is not poor."

"I didn't think of it until you asked me."

"After the attack, did you hear him run away?"

"Yes, he ran back into the alley–but I couldn't see–"

"Were his steps quick and sure. Did he shuffle? Was there anything unique about the sound of his running?"

"No, but he ran very quickly. He was gone in an instant."

"Then he is a man in good physical condition. We can surmise that much for now. Well, his behavior is certainly unusual for a thief. If robbery was his motive he certainly had every opportunity to take your possessions. What about the second attack against you?"

"Th-There's no doubt the second attack was a deliberate attempt to kill me." The diminutive man here twisted and wrung his hands, his distress rising to the surface once more. "It occurred only last night. It was terrible, Mr. Hawkes. Frightened me half out of my wits. It–"

"Please, calm down. State only the facts. What happened?"

"Yes, sorry. The time–was nearing eight o'clock in the evening. I was sitting in my chair next to a lamp, reading as I normally do. I'm an avid reader. As I sat absorbed in the book I was startled by the sound of a rifle retort. The window nearby shattered to bits, some pieces of glass hitting me, falling down

19

upon me. Someone had taken a shot at me! I was so stunned that at first I was unable to believe it. I still find it hard to believe! I sat staring at my shattered window for a few seconds and then, realizing what had occurred, I dropped to the floor. There I waited, crouching in a perfect agony of fear. I thought he'd shoot again, or come bursting through my door into my home to finish me. It was only a minute or two but it seemed a lifetime. I'm a nervous man by nature, Mr. Hawkes, and this was, and is, almost unendurable to me."

There was something so very pitiable in Dunmore's tone, and the constant wringing of his hands, that even Simon, normally little more than an automaton of rationality at such times, was momentarily moved to compassion for the man as he sat opposite him.

"Finally," concluded Dunmore, "I crawled out of the room, on my hands and knees. Afraid to stand in my own home! It was terrible, Mr. Hawkes. Terrible!"

"You're doing well. Please, a few more questions. Your window, does it face the street?"

"Yes, I read in a front room of my home."

"Hum, then it is highly likely, with the possibility of a passerby coming along, that the shooter fired from the privacy of a roof or a room across the street opposite you." Simon passed his hand over his chin. "Of course you reported this event to the police as well. What did they discover?"

"Ah, no–no Mr. Hawkes, I didn't report it."

Simon was surprised. "No? Why not?"

"Because, Mr. Hawkes, I-I'm afraid of scandal. Last night, last night it suddenly occurred to me that the attacker–the attacker might very well be my own brother." Dunmore's face here twisted with sorrow. "My own brother–"

"Go on," urged Hawkes. "Pray tell me why you would suspect your brother."

"Oh, if I'm wrong. I'll be so ashamed for suspecting him. But who else? Who else?"

"Why do you suspect him?" repeated Simon.

"My brother–is a man of intelligence and talent, which he has decided to waste. He is fourteen years younger than I am. He turned twenty-eight just last August. When he was twenty-one he inherited a good income, the benefit of a trust set up for him by our father. He had a remarkable career at Harvard and seemed poised for a successful life. But after college he threw himself into a life of play, of debauchery. He went to all the fashionable places and was very extravagant with his money. I thought it a phase he'd pass through but it only became increasingly worse. He's now–little more than a fornicator, a gambler and a drunkard."

"A harsh indictment–but it doesn't explain why you believe he would attempt to kill you."

"He needs money. The trust is recently gone, depleted. He's my sole legal heir. Upon my death he would inherit all I have. I understand his gambling losses to be exceeding any ability he has to pay them."

"Despite your recent setbacks, I take it that the amount he would inherit remains considerable."

Dunmore blinked his surprise and then stared at him. "My setbacks? Why, why, how do you know that? I've told no one. You're right though, I've suffered some losses in my investments and the others I cannot touch for the time. I've even hired myself out as a clerk for some months, copying documents mostly, to earn some funds to get me over a hump. I just recently resigned from that position. But my brother is unaware of any of that–and still, even so, he'd inherit enough to keep him in women and drink for a long time. There is enough to allow him to continue to do nothing of worth, to continue to waste his life, for quite a while. I don't understand him. He really is a superior intelligence. I don't understand why he squanders the abilities God has granted him. I have tried to dissuade him from his current life, but to no avail. I've even ventured into that low eatery he lunches at when his funds are low, a saloon called The Jolly Pigeon on Cherry Street–"

"The Jolly Pigeon, I'm aware of it," broke in Hawkes.

"Then you know. The place is rough. A bit frightening to me. But I went. I thought if I talked to him there, while he was actually sitting in the type of low place his life choices were bringing him to, I could convince him to change. To better himself. He simply laughed at me." Dunmore sank into thoughtfulness for a moment before piping up again, "Oh, don't be concerned, Mr. Hawkes. I can certainly pay you for your troubles. No worry about that."

Hawkes waved the words off. "Don't give a thought to that. We can always work out something. Your brother, is he proficient with firearms?"

"Yes, he is, or at least was, a good shot. When he was in college he practiced a great deal."

"Hum, the obvious. Have you given any thought to changing your will?"

"Mr. Hawkes, I have only suspicions. I could be wrong about him. I pray to God I am! I won't change my will until I'm certain it's he who is at fault. That's why I need you. If it is him I will not press any charges. I don't want the police involved if that proves to be the case. I don't want him publicly disgraced and imprisoned. I just want him to know that I know, and that he will not benefit from his crime. That should suffice to stop him. God, I do hope it proves not to be him! But if not him, then who? It explains the first attack. Perhaps he intended to kill me but relented because I'm his brother. Relented at that moment in any case, only to have his need–reassert itself again later. Oh, who else could it be? I haven't an enemy in the world. I keep entirely to myself." Dunmore's struggle to maintain stoically his composure began to falter once again and fear and anxiousness once more crept into his rasping voice. "God, this is insanity! Who else would do this to me? Who!"

"Calm yourself. That is precisely what must be discovered."

"Forgive me. I'm so frightened. To suddenly find myself in the midst of this dreadful situation. I couldn't sleep last night. Today, leaving my home and going to Hammond's house, and then coming here, every street seemed to hold the possibility of death for me. I was unable to hail a cab and walked. Every corner, every door seemed to possess potential danger. I imagined an assassin to be lurking in every shadow. It's terrifying! Terrifying!"

"Terrifying–and interesting," responded Hawkes, springing to his feet as he gave voice simultaneously to a commiseration for the pain of the man's terror and his enthusiasm over the puzzle being presented to him. "There is indeed a mystery hanging over you and there may be some novelty here. It is interesting. I will endeavour to do what I can to resolve it. I remind you that I have promised my time to another as well, and so I will not be able to devote myself entirely to your cause. Is that acceptable to you?"

Dunmore replied that it was.

"Come then, let us go to your home and see what we can discover there."

Dunmore's expression transformed to one of sheer gratitude. "You will help. Oh, thank you, Mr. Hawkes. I don't know what I would have done if you refused." Following Hawkes lead, he started up out of his chair, but then, in the next instant, immediately sank back into it again. In living through the terror of the night and in walking the streets in fear of his life to go first to Hammond's home and then to seek out Simon Hawkes, he'd depleted the small reservoir of mettle available to him. Now he found he had no courage remaining to allow him to return to his own home. "I-I'm not a brave man, Mr. Hawkes. Please don't think poorly of me if I tell you–I'm not up to going back. I-I can't. Not yet–"

"I understand. You do look done-in. Let me have the number and street of your home. It might be better if I go on my own in any case. I'll need your house key in order to allow me inside. In the meantime, you might think about getting yourself some rest. Feel free to utilize the bed here if you wish."

"Thank you. It's very kind. I think however I might obtain a room of my own. Perhaps I will remain here–for a day or two in any case."

"Good. That may be wise," responded Hawkes, digging a Mackintosh out of his portmanteau and slipping his arms through the sleeves, putting it on to serve as protection against the drizzle outside. "Do you know if your brother is low on his luck and funds at the moment?" he asked. "If so, I may try to seek him out at the Pigeon."

"He came to me for money, just hours before the shooting. So, yes, he must be."

"Good. I'm off then." With these three words serving as his *adieu*, Hawkes went out of the room and was gone, leaving Franklin Dunmore blinking his red-rimmed, tired eyes at the abruptness of the departure.

CHAPTER FIVE

Dunmore's townhouse was a three-story brick with some charm, one in the midst of a row of similar houses, all sitting sullen now in the grey of the dreary morning. Even if Hawkes had not been given the number of the house, 327, he'd have easily pinpointed the Dunmore home by the presence of the broken window on the first floor immediately to the left of the entrance as you approach the house. Directly across the street was a squat apartment building of four floors.

Inside, a few steps along a narrow passageway brought him to the parlor entrance, the parlor being the room in which Dunmore was sitting and reading when the shot had been fired. Here, Hawkes saw furniture of some quality, purchased prior to Dunmore's current financial problems. The floor was a herringbone parquet, covered in part in the centre by an Oriental rug beginning to show signs of wear. The armchair next to the window through which the bullet had entered was a distance from the hearth but not so far a sitter wouldn't benefit from the fire. Next to the armchair was another chair, a straight-backed one, which, as evidenced by the few books laying on it, served the function of a side table rather than that for which it was created. A clock on the mantelpiece showed the time. The fire had long ago gone out, and the open drapes and broken window had admitted the cold night air so that the room was filled with the chill and damp of the weather outside. The interior sill of the window and the floor underneath was wet with rain.

On the floor, near the armchair, was the volume being read by Dunmore and dropped on the floor when the shot was fired. Hawkes went and picked it up: a copy of Stevenson's *The Strange Case of Doctor Jekyll and Mr. Hyde*. Hawkes was familiar with it. The book was just making its appearance here in the States, but had, five or six years earlier, created a sensation in England.

25

Hawkes put the book down with the others on the straight-backed chair and sat in the armchair, sinking low into its comfort. Dunmore's head and shoulders would have been visible through the window, but no higher than the lower pane of glass. It was the upper pane that'd been shattered by the bullet. "Very wide in his shot," murmured Hawkes.

Pushing himself out of the chair, he strode to the wall opposite the window and let his sharp eyes scan the surface until he found what he was looking for. Producing a pocket knife, he dug the bullet out of the wall, studied it for a few seconds as it lay in the palm of his hand and then dropped it into his pocket as he returned to the window, his mind already drawing an imaginary line from shattered pane to the bullet hole in the wall. Standing at the window, he extended that line directly to the roofline of the building across the street. The sound of horses hooves echoed in the air as a horse and buggy trotted by on the street outside.

Years later, as Holmes related these facts to me, very matter-of-fact as is his manner when speaking of his own experiences, I envisioned the transformation occurring in him in Dunmore's home that I had witnessed so often previously in his demeanor at such moments. As I have stated in previous writings, there was more than the thinker, the logician, involved at these moments. His eyes hardened, his lips compressed and there arose in him a purely instinctual and animal-like lust for the hunt. While Holmes himself stressed the scientific aspects of the skills of observation and deduction of which he was, and is, so rightly proud, he failed to realize that there was as much deep-seeded emotion involved in his activities as well. He hated the idea of this, did Holmes, and any time I suggested it to him, would angrily wave my comments away.

Although then concealing himself under the alias of Simon Hawkes, he was still Sherlock Holmes and, as he related the facts to me, I could envision him in my mind's eye striding purposely out of the house and crossing the street to the apartment house that was now his focus, his face set like stone, his keen eyes flashing like that of a tiger catching the scent of prey floating on the wind and seeking sight of it, that prey, so that it could be brought down by the claws of justice.

The apartment building was, as stated previously, a relatively modest sized one of just four levels. A thin alley ran between it and its neighbour to the left. On the right it touched against another apartment building also of four landings but slightly shorter in overall height. The roof was, in part, obscured from view as a portion of it was cloaked by the interlacing branches of two trees that stood in front of the building. The foliage wasn't thick but provided convenient enough cover for the shooter, judged Hawkes as he glanced up at the branches. At night, a man would be virtually invisible, in the darkness and behind the tree branches, to anyone who might be passing on the street below, even if one happened to cast one's gaze up to the roof. The street was narrow and not heavily trafficked, certainly with nowhere near the amount of pedestrian and carriage traffic present on the avenues with which it intersected at either end.

Hawkes went through the building entrance, stepping first into a small foyer area and then, passing through a second door, into a narrow hall. It was empty, dimly lit, and no one was present to question his presence. The passageway ran to the rear of the building to a flight of stairs. It will be necessary to question the tenants, Hawkes decided as he walked the length of the shadowed hall, on the fortuitous chance that someone may have seen a stranger in the building the previous night.

The stairs, trampled and mucked up by the steps of the tenants in the morning, offered him nothing of interest. Hawkes ascended to the top and found himself standing before the door that opened onto the roof. Examining it, he again was disappointed to find naught that would be of help to him. Attempting to open the aged door, he found it resisted him at first. Pushing harder, it opened, creaking on old and rusting hinges, and he stepped through onto the roof.

Here he immediately produced his lens and scrutinized the rooftop, focusing his attention upon that side of the roof that

27

faced the Dunmore house. Almost immediately he discovered a spent cartridge shell. Yes, it was here the shooter crouched to take his shot. A low wall of brick went around the roof, just three feet in height. Against a piece of brick, Hawkes saw through his lens a fresh smudge of boot polish, black, where the toe of a boot had rubbed against the wall. After another quarter-hour of examination, he determined there was nothing else to be discovered.

The cartridge revealed information. A .44 Russian cartridge unless he was off the mark, used in the Smith & Wesson .44, a popular weapon in the States and a pistol that could be purchased with a detachable shoulder stock, allowing the owner to convert it into a passable carbine when necessity required it. A hinged-frame model using an automatic ejecting system. The pistol was designed in America but the cartridge it used was created by the Russians to grant the pistol greater accuracy and longer distance. Subsequent to improving the design of the bullet, they ordered thousands of the weapon for their own army.

Simon, placing the cartridge into his pocket beside the bullet it had fired, went to the roof's edge once again and gazed across the street. Despite the trees there was a clear view of the Dunmore house. Not a difficult shot with a Smith & Wesson. Dunmore was indeed fortunate to be alive. He took in and exhaled a deep breath of the damp air, maintaining the tautness of the hunter's aspect he'd assumed only minutes earlier. There was a tranquility here on the rooftop above the city streets, a sense of separation from the turmoil of the human activity on the streets below. It was unnoticed by Hawkes.

It was more likely than not, he decided, that the shooter did not go back through the roof door after taking his shot at Dunmore. Perhaps the fire-escape on the back of the building? No, it was more probable that he would use that on the adjacent building. It would be a simple matter for a man to go from this roof to the one beside it. Acting upon this supposition, Hawkes went to the roof's edge where it overlooked the top of the next building. This roof was a few feet higher but a relatively easy leap would conquer the distance. Yes, there it was, a recently made scrape where someone landed after jumping down. Even at this distance Hawkes' sharp eyes could see it. The shooter had indeed made his exit this way. Hawkes made the leap himself, his unbuttoned Mackintosh flaring up behind him as he fell, making him appear for an instant like a great giant-winged bird of prey, and landed easily on the roof below. He walked to the fire-escape leading down to a yard in the back and descended it. Reaching the ground below, he produced his magnifying glass and, going down on his haunches, brought his eager eyes and the lens they peered through near the moist earth. Yes, there were the indentations in the ground made by the shooter's boots when he dropped to the ground. Square-toed boots. Hawkes produced a pocket tape-measure now as well, using it to measure the distance between the tracks. He then made an examination of the path from beneath the fire-escape to where the yard met the alley. After a few minutes, he was satisfied he'd seen all there was to see that could be of assistance to him and left the yard, going to the alley and making his way to the sidewalk. It was time to begin to knock on doors. Perhaps someone in the building from which the shot had been fired witnessed the presence of a stranger last night and, if that stranger was the same person as the shooter, he might obtain a description of Franklin Dunmore's would-be and so far inefficient killer. If so, the case might very well resolve itself into simplicity after all.

CHAPTER SIX

Hawkes, foregoing use of a cab and returning to The Dead Rabbits Society on foot, stopped only once in his walk, at a tobacco bureau to obtain a sufficient amount of shag tobacco in preparation for an afternoon of contemplation. On the avenues, there was activity everywhere. The street merchants displayed their wares beneath awnings outside their shops and peddlers stood near the kerbs to hawk their wares. Most of the avenues had retail shops on the ground floor with apartments above. The streets here served as places of mercantile activity during the day and of distraction at night when the places of entertainment they held, the small theaters, beer gardens, and oyster saloons, dominated. Acting on impulse, Hawkes passed by Prince Street and continued his way downtown, finding himself, as he'd done more than once previously, exploring and familiarizing himself with the streets of the American city. It was so like London in many respects, even in its slums. Hawkes, never one to avoid the squalid section of a city, indeed many times seeking them out, soon turned a corner and entered onto streets of poverty, penetrating into the boundaries of the area in New York City known as "the Bend". It was located in the unsavory "Bloody Sixth" Ward of the city very near a section proclaimed with less than affection as "Bandits' Roost". Hawkes now strode past decaying buildings, rows of five-story tenements that sat side by side beneath a long common roof and small shacks that more resembled cowsheds than places of human habitation. Here soot and filth rather than sunlight coated the facades of the buildings and here too many poor souls sought refuge within boundaries already filled to bursting with squalor and decay. Immigrants, mostly Celtic and Italian, a few Chinese, existed here alongside the despair that seemed to lurk everywhere, in the darkened halls of the buildings and in the eyes of many of the tenants. The mortality rate of the city was driven higher by the presence of these tenements and the diseases they invited. Cholera and influenza were no strangers here. Women hurried by, most carrying loads of some kind or another. Either a bundle of fire-wood on their heads or a small pile of days-old decaying vegetables in a pouch made by folding their aprons. The aging food, just hours away from being declared inedible, being all they could afford to purchase. Some women nursed immodestly, a baby sitting at their breast held in place by a cloth sling to prevent the infant from falling and, at the same time, allowing the arms and hands the freedom to work. Most of the mothers appeared to be little more than children themselves. There was a dearth of polite gentlemen here as the women did most of the carrying, indeed they appeared to do most of the work being performed in the Bend. The men, for the most part, sat or stood in the streets, on carts or in the open doors of the saloons, smoking their clay pipes and talking with each other. It reminded Hawkes of London's East End and he had no doubt that, as in the London slum, murder and crime were fruits that grew more abundantly out of the soil here than elsewhere. Hawkes found his right hand nestling very near the small pistol he carried with him in the pocket of his Macintosh. At the same time he felt sympathy for the bulk of the inhabitants here in this filthy section of the city. Immigrants for the most part, they traveled here to America to find a dream and found themselves instead taken advantage of, used and mistreated. It was their poverty, their need, their sad existence in these less than adequate living conditions, that drove them, some of them in any case, to their dissolute behavior and, in that regard, they were as much victims as those they committed crimes against. It would be a test of civic responsibility, of governmental conscience, to clean up these slums and many voices were already shouting for government action to be taken. Still, it was a mistake to allow sympathy to make one careless.

Hawkes had come here for no reason that could be attached to Franklin Dunmore's problem, but rather out of simple curiosity, having read an article in the Times a few days earlier

31

in which the more unsavory areas of the city, "the Bend", "the Tenderloin District" and the "Five Points", were described in detail. The reporter had quoted passages from the book by Jacob Riis, "How the Other Half Lives", and, to Hawkes' mind, neither reporter nor Riis had exaggerated in their portraits of these sections, not of "the Bend", in any case. The book would be suitably read in London as well.

His continued excursion soon brought him entirely through the unpalatable, crowded and fetid streets and back again to an area that spoke more of well-being and prosperity. He was walking back uptown, once again going towards Prince Street and The Dead Rabbits Society. Here his mind returned to his investigation of the attempts upon Franklin Dunmore's life.

His examination of Dunmore's room and of the rooftop opposite the house had provided some information, and inspired a few new questions as well. He'd spent the last two hours in the apartment building going from flat to flat and interviewing the tenants. Here he enjoyed a bit of fortune. One of the residents, an elderly, grey-haired woman living on the third floor, recalled seeing a stranger in the building the previous night. She caught sight of the man's back as he ascended the stairs at the end of the hall. Unfortunately she had not seen his face at all. He was a man, she told him, who was well over six feet in height (in this particular instance, she was inaccurate, decided Hawkes immediately) who carried himself with "a distinguished air about him". He wore a bowler and a long dark overcoat. She offered the stranger little thought at the time as he carried with him, in his right hand, a medical bag and she assumed he was a doctor making a call.

A little additional investigation had proven that assumption incorrect.

Hawkes was certain that this man was the same person pursuing Franklin Dunmore. Clever that, carrying the medical bag with him.

What was the motive here? Why was this man hunting Dunmore? The purpose behind the attacks remained as obscure as ever. If they were not the work of Charles Dunmore, motivated by his need for money, then who? And if someone else, then why? It was this question, the pondering of the purpose of the two attempts of murder against the seemingly harmless man, that sat upon Hawkes' mind as he entered once again through the heavy, carved wooden doors of The Dead Rabbits Society.

An inquiry with the desk-clerk confirmed that Dunmore had done what earlier he had said he would do: acquire lodging at the Society. Hawkes obtained the room number and had started up the stairs to go to it when he changed his mind. It was just a bit past eleven and it was possible that the man had gone to his bed to catch up on his sleep. If so it was repose he desperately needed, worn with fear and exhaustion as he was. Best to let him slumber for the time.

The shouts and yells he then heard above him changed his mind on the instant. He recognized immediately the voice of Franklin Dunmore. The man was screaming in holy terror as though his last moment of life was being snatched away from him.

CHAPTER SEVEN

Hawkes raced up the stairs, taking them two at a time with his long legs, and was on the third floor in moments. A distance down the corridor he saw Dunmore, clad in pants and shirt and shoeless, his black hair unkempt from being pressed against his bed pillow. Dunmore's eyes fell upon him in the next moment and he came towards him, the embodiment of fear, more staggering than walking, his mouth attempting to form words of speech. Then he abruptly fell to the floor where he lay insensate as Hawkes ran to him.

Leaning down towards the prostrate form of the man, Hawkes placed his fingertips to his neck. There he was able to detect a strong pulse. Hawkes' fear for the man's life was immediately put to rest. Franklin Dunmore had simply fainted dead away.

The door to Dunmore's room remained open and Hawkes went through it. Inside he saw the reason for Dunmore's screams. There, hanging from a bedpost, was a gruesome sight, a black cat, its throat cut and its front coated with dried blood, its lips curled back in its own terror as though attempting to snarl at the very death that now held it in its grip. Waking to that grisly carcass, it was no wonder the agitated and apprehensive man reacted as he did.

It was an unmistakable message to Dunmore, a mocking continuation of the threat against him. Hawkes studied the carcass. An alley cat, its battle scars spoke of a life on the street. It'd been killed hours earlier. The rope that was strung around its neck was common thick cord, purchasable almost anywhere. The knots too were common. Little to discover here. And yet there was something to learn. The presence of the cat was suggestive. It did no less than confirm the suspicion Hawkes had carried with him during his excursion through "the Bend". Dunmore's assailant was indeed playing a cat and mouse game with the

34

man. The attempts against Dunmore's life had failed only because the attacker wanted them to fail.

On the small table beside the bed sat a bottle of laudanum and a wine-glass. No doubt Dunmore had obtained the laudanum from a pharmacist to aid in his sleep. If he'd taken a strong dose of it, then it would explain how someone was able to enter his room without waking the man.

Hawkes removed a pillow from the bed and returned with it to the fallen Dunmore. Others had appeared in the hall by now and were standing about the prostrate man. One of the men was George Hammond. "Hawkes!" he exclaimed, seeing the detective emerge from Dunmore's room with the pillow. "Good heavens man, what's happened here? Is Frank all right? Has he been hurt?"

"He's all right," responded Hawkes, going down on his haunches once again to place the pillow beneath Dunmore's head. "Nothing a spot of brandy and rest won't cure."

Dunmore's eyelids quivered and then fluttered open. He stared through dazed and overwrought eyes up at Hawkes. "D-Did you s-see...? In my room..."

"Yes, yes. How are you? Can you stand?"

Dunmore's face coloured a bit with shame as he realized his position. Immediately he began to push himself up from the floor. "I'm dreadfully sorry. I-I've overreacted—"

Hammond reached out an arm and he and Hawkes assisted the now embarrassed man to his feet. "Come," said Hammond, "we'll get you back to your room."

"N-No!" protested Dunmore. "No, I can't go back in there." The flush in his face evaporated and he was nothing but chalk-like pallor once more.

"My room is right here," said Hawkes. "Come, you can rest there for the time. I'll order a brandy for you."

Dunmore turned to Hawkes, his hand suddenly gripping the detective's forearm tightly, an infusion of sudden strength generated by his fear. "He's come here! After me! He's come here!"

"Yes," replied Hawkes softly, leading the shaken man to his room. "Yes, that's so." Dunmore responded to Hawkes' words with a dismal groan.

Hawkes, aided by Hammond, supported Dunmore as he led him to his bed. The terrified man collapsed heavily into it, the bedsprings squealing with even his slight weight. Deciding that the laudanum would be more effective at the moment than the previously suggested brandy, Hawkes requested Hammond to retrieve the bottle from Dunmore's room. Minutes after taking a dose of the drug, Dunmore closed his eyes and sank once again into a deep and much needed sleep. How long it would last, given the man's state, was questionable.

Hawkes took a moment to remove his Mackintosh and drop it over the back of a chair, then he and Hammond withdrew with Hawkes locking the door behind him.

CHAPTER EIGHT

"**I**'ve interviewed the desk-clerk," stated Hawkes as he pulled a chair from the table and placed himself it. "He saw nothing that struck him as unusual. Just the usual delivery men and club members arriving in the lobby."

"I feel sorry for him," stated Hammond, speaking of Dunmore now as he too seated himself at the table. The two men, both not having eaten since breaking their fast in the morning, had decided to lunch together in the Dead Rabbits. "He's really not up to this. The man's in wretched shape."

"I fear that's so," replied Hawkes.

"In God's name, what's happening to him? He came to me early this morning in a state. I swear he was babbling so I had to get him to calm down to get his story out of him. Someone was trying to kill him he said! I wanted to call in the police but to my amazement he ordered me not to do it. In the end I suggested he go to you, which advice I must assume he accepted."

A waiter came over to them and both men put in their order. "He did," stated Hawkes after the waiter had gone. "Early this morning, right after speaking to you."

"Well, the police will be involved now. I believe the desk-clerk has summoned them."

"They'll be told of what appears to be little more than a cruel prank. I doubt Dunmore will want to tell them of the shooting attack against him, and until he releases me to do so, I will not break his trust. I request that you honour the man's wishes as well. At least for now."

"Why for heavens sake? Why not tell the police?"

"He wants to be certain his brother is not behind the attacks. If so, he doesn't want a scandal, and, believe it or not, he retains enough familial love for his brother that he doesn't want to see him sent to prison. Not even if evidence reveals it is his brother doing this to him."

Hammond leaned back in his chair. "Is that so?"

"Those are his wishes as stated to me."

"He's a better man than me. I'd see my brother on a gallows if he tried to kill me. If I had a brother that is."

"Most would do the same. Still it's his preference I'm speaking of and not that of others."

"All right, Mr. Hawkes. I too will respect his wishes. I suppose he deserves to have us give them some regard. Have you had a chance to look into his–situation? Have you learned anything that would pin this on Charlie?"

"I confess to a certain amount of puzzlement. The closer one looks–" Hawkes voice trailed off and he was silent for a moment before continuing. "After speaking to Dunmore I went first to his house and then to the roof of the building across the street. It was from there the shot was fired into his home. I can say this about our man. He is, I judge, a man approximately five-ten in height and in good trim, weighing about one-eighty. He is in possession of a Smith & Wesson .44, the weapon used on the roof. He is a gentleman in his bearing who is at least somewhat fastidious in his appearance as he took the time to recently polish his black boots. Square-toed boots by the way. He is right-handed, intelligent and cunning. And unusually cautious. After taking his shot at Dunmore, he left the roof not the same way he came, but rather over the rooftop of the adjacent building, dropping down into a yard and then walking out the alley. This put him a distance away from the crime by the time he made his appearance on the pavement."

Hammond blinked at the detective and gazed at him with amazement on his features. "Why, sir, that's remarkable. How in the world did you discover all that?"

"It is simplicity itself," replied Hawkes. "On the roof I discovered a recently discarded cartridge shell, a .44 Russian cartridge used commonly in the Smith & Wesson. I saw also a fresh smudge of boot polish on the wall of the roof facing Dunmore's home. It was left there by our shooter, left behind when the toe of his polished boot scraped the wall as he leaned forward to take his shot. As to his weight and height, it is a simple matter to calculate that data through the tracks a person leaves behind. Our man left very clear prints in the yard through which he walked. I did obtain a description of the height and size of the man from a woman in the building who happened to see him. He was posing as a medical man, going up the stairs to the roof. Unfortunately, she saw only his back and so could not describe his features to me. He held the medical bag he carried with him in his right hand. She put him at 'well over six foot' but I'm inclined to believe she misjudged in that regard. She was rather short in height herself and there is a tendency for short people to over-estimate the height of others. It occurs quite often. No, the hard data, the impressions of his tracks in the earth put him nearer five foot and ten and I will accept the hard data as the truth."

"My goodness–someone saw him," murmured Hammond. "Yes, it's too bad this woman didn't see his face. But wait, this man she saw carried a medical bag you said. Perhaps he was simply what he appeared to be, a doctor making a call to a patient. That could be, couldn't it? The woman said he was taller than you believe the shooter to be. So what makes you think this particular man and Dunmore's assailant are one and the same? The man could just be a doctor."

"No, that can't be. The woman lives on the third of four floors in the building. Since the doctor was seen going up to the next floor, the summons, if there was one, would have had to come from one of the tenants on the fourth floor. I simply talked to each tenant on that floor. Each denied calling a physician. Their denials were amply supported by the fact that all on the floor were as healthy as horses. No, the physician is our man. It was resourceful, his using the doctor's bag to lend him an air of respectable purpose for being in the building. It afforded him acceptance there even though a stranger."

"How did you suspect he went over to the next rooftop? Why it seems to me the man would want to go straight out the way he came. It'd be faster."

Philip J. Carraher

"Perhaps he heard someone on the stairs when he started to leave the roof. Our man is astute enough to know that there would be more interest paid to a stranger, even one presenting himself as a medical man, following an unusual event such as the sound of a gunshot, rather than before. Anyone hearing the gunshot would have their sense of alertness driven up and would be quite naturally wondering at its cause. If people then saw him leaving the building, they would place more emphasis upon his presence there. They would be apt to study him more closely than previously. Perhaps he intended to leave via the fire-escape all along. Whatever the reason, that is the means he chose to leave. I suspected as much immediately. When I went to the roof, I found the door leading to it closed and it required a bit of an effort to open it as its hinges were old and rusted. If our man had left this way, the door more likely would have been left open as he would not want to waste precious time to pull it closed. There was also no reason to close it upon leaving while he would almost certainly close it when first stepping onto the roof. He'd do this in order to assure his privacy as he took his place there to fire his shot. Acting on that reasoning I assumed he went down the fire-escape. Then, judging he'd want to put as much distance between him and the point of his crime as quickly as possible, I thought it very reasonable that he would choose to go to the next roof and use that building's fire-escape. That subsequently proved to be the case. If I'd been wrong I would have gone back to the other fire-escape and picked up his trail there."

"Why didn't he first go up to the roof the same way? Why go through the building at all?"

"The leap from the ground to the fire-escape's ladder is a difficult one. To drop down from it to the ground is a simple matter. Also, as I said, his use of the fire-escape may have been an impromptu one. He may not have originally intended to use it at all."

"It's wonderful the way you've thought it all out. My word, as much credit as you give him for being clever, there's even more cleverness on your part, it seems to me, in regards to the

40

way you ferreted out all that information from such scraps. Even correcting the woman's eyewitness account. I doubt our police would be capable of it. Still, the description you realized through your work is not all that helpful when all is said and done, is it? I mean it fits almost half the men in New York. It fits his brother Charlie as well."

"It serves at least to exclude the other half. It eliminates Franklin Dunmore, for example."

"Frank Dunmore! But it's he—"

"It was a thought I never took seriously," interrupted Hawkes. "That he might be staging these attacks against himself for some unknown reason. Still it was an idea that was there and it's nice not to have to consider it any longer."

Their food was then placed before them and each man devoted himself for the next minute or so to sampling their respective meals.

"I will suggest," said Hawkes, breaking the silence, "that he obtain a bodyguard. Someone he can trust to stay at his side. I hope he doesn't refuse although I fear he may. He prizes his privacy too much."

"Maybe Frank would be safer out of town for a time, while you look for the man who is after him. Would it be helpful if I offered him a place to stay? Out of the city? I'm going to be leaving the day after tomorrow, going up to Black Oak, my country house upstate near the Grand Hotel, to get a breath of country air. I've invited some friends there too. He's welcome to come along. It might throw this fiend off who is hounding him and the time out of the city may do his health some good as well."

Hawkes brow furrowed as he digested the offer. "His nerves could use a respite from all of this, no doubt. If Watso— if I was a medical man I might recommend it. Still, for your own sake I would argue against making the offer. It might prove dangerous. Whoever it is who is hunting him has followed him here to the Society. He may very well follow him to your country house as well."

Hammond waved away Hawkes words. "It's one thing to be aware of a man's movements within the area of a few city blocks and quite another to track him out of the city. Besides there'll be ample protection in the house in the form of my own pistol and in my servants. Especially my new man, Braxton. He's my livery man, and an ex-prizefighter. Once he fought twenty-five rounds with Sullivan. He's got the mug to show for it too. His face alone would act as a deterrent to anyone with sense. And he's a dead shot." Hammond took a bite of food and then continued. "Certainly Frank would be safer surrounded by people rather than remaining alone."

Hawkes grunted. "How long will you be gone?"

"Two weeks. Three perhaps. No longer. After that, the trees start to close in on me. My wife stays there longer. She enjoys the summers there. If you remain concerned, maybe you would like to come along as well?"

"Thank you but no," replied Hawkes. "I have a commitment which obligates me to remain here. I have been remiss in ignoring it today for the benefit of looking into Dunmore's problem."

"Are you giving up on finding this man hunting Frank?"

"Without more facts there is nothing more I can do. If the pistol were a less common one, I would consider going round to the local gun shops in an endeavour to determine the names of purchasers, but such is not the case. No, until I have more to go on, I will be unable to proceed any further."

"I will lay you odds," said Hammond, placing a tone of insistence into his voice, "that when all is said and done, Charlie Dunmore proves to be your boy. He's after his brother's money, pure and simple."

"That may be so. It is certainly possible."

A clock sounded the hour, chiming in the adjoining room. Hawkes pushed his meal away, leaving it half-eaten and pushed himself from the table "My apologies, I must be going. Have them bill the cost of our food to my room. Good day." He took only two steps from the table before turning around again. "Your

42

thought of extending an invitation to Dunmore, to ask him to join you as a guest in your country home, is a generous one, an act of kindness that does you credit, but again I suggest it is a gesture you may want to reconsider. There is danger pursuing the man and it may be wiser to listen to the voice of caution rather than one of compassion."

Hammond smiled and once again waved away Hawkes' concern. "No need for worry. We'll be fine," he responded dismissively. "Its not the nature of criminals to strike when there are crowds about. Not in my experience. I trust not in yours as well. And if I don't extend the invitation to him now, having thought of it, and he subsequently comes to harm left on his own here in the city, I would feel it to be partly my fault. No, don't worry. We'll be fine."

Hawkes nodded his head. "I understand. Be careful then."

"Nothing will happen," responded Hammond. "Nothing. I'm confident of it." He spoke now with a certitude that Hawkes could only hope would not ultimately prove to be misplaced. "In any case, I and some members of my household staff are well armed and perfectly capable of defending ourselves should the need arise. We'll be fine."

"Very well then," returned Hawkes. "I will see you again upon your return." With those parting words, he turned and walked away, carrying with him the unsettling thought that, in his experience and all too often, such elevated confidence as that exhibited by George Hammond subsequently proved to be nothing less than a prelude to devastation and grief.

CHAPTER NINE

As stated by Franklin Dunmore, it was the habit of his brother, when low on funds, to take his midday meal in a small eatery and saloon dubbed "The Jolly Pigeon", the sobriquet obtained due to the number of birds that feasted on discarded crumbs immediately outside its entrance. It was a small establishment located on Cherry Street near Blindman's Alley which was another sobriquet, the "alley" obtaining its name from a colony of blind beggars being housed in the tenement there, one of many tenements located in the midst of a swarming poverty not unlike "the Bend".

The Pigeon offered a serving of edible food at a price that caused little strain to the purse and it was there that Charles Dunmore, his pride acquiescing to his hunger, suffered himself to dine among the riff-raff he deplored. Delmonico's, his preference for dining, and the "swells" who there enjoyed the exquisite food of Chef Ranhofer, might have existed in a different country from this eatery, which, in a significant way, it did. There was some miniscule comfort for those dining at the Pigeon in their knowing that at least, however low a rung on the ladder of society they stood, they were steps above the absolute bottom, the dregs of the city. The lowest rung was left to the beer-dives and two-cent restaurants, existing primarily in "the Bend". These were the places frequented by society's dregs, not by choice but by necessity, as those eating in such dens simply could not afford to eat elsewhere. Charles Dunmore was certain he would never sink so low as to eat in such rat-holes. In his youth and lack of personal experience he didn't realize that, in his having to dine in such a place as the Pigeon at all, he was as a man crossing a lake on a sheet of thawing ice, in danger of crashing through to the ultimate low circumstances he was so proud of eluding. Once fallen through, he, like most others who found themselves in the unforgiving grasp of extreme poverty, would find it difficult to climb out and would in all likelihood instead drown in its deep cruel waters. He always carried with him, while walking on Cherry Street and in the surrounding area, and while dining at the Pigeon, a pistol for protection in the pocket of his coat.

Hawkes, made aware of Charles Dunmore's habit during the course of conversation with his brother, made his way to The Jolly Pigeon immediately after departing his lunch with George Hammond. The Pigeon consisted of one good-sized room serving drink and food and another smaller room, the kitchen, in the back. The main room was dark, with only one shaded and grime-covered window. The grime (primarily on the outside) of such thickness that even the brightest sunlight failed to summon the strength to push through it. The darkness of the interior was relieved by two feeble gaslights, one on either side of the room. The bar was on the right, and consisted of a few barrels over which two wide planks of smooth wood were placed. Behind it were some shelves holding an array of bottles containing varieties of drink. A mirror was placed on the wall behind the bar as well and sat gleaming like a great eye peering out from the midst of the many bottles. Other than that single ornamentation the walls of the place were left bare. Tables were placed in a seemingly haphazard fashion all about the room, some pressed very close together. The rough timber of the floor was covered with fresh sawdust. The room, to the owner's credit, was kept as clean as possible. A sullen hush was the atmosphere that pervaded the place when Hawkes made his appearance. The customers of The Jolly Pigeon seemed for the most part to eat their food as though entering into a business transaction, a task to be gotten through rather than enjoyed. It was different at night, more boisterous and loud, when the serious drinkers and dipsomaniacs arrived.

Hawkes obtained a pint at the bar and went to a table, the size of which was barely sufficient to hold his glass, near the window. There he produced his pipe, lit it up and waited. His patience was rewarded within the half-hour as, in the midst of reaching for more tobacco for his pipe, he saw Charles Dunmore enter and place himself at a slightly larger table on the opposite side of the room.

Hawkes put away his pipe and waited until Dunmore had made his order, a lunch consisting of cabbage and potatoes drenched in vinegar, before walking over and introducing himself. The young man, his eyes widening in surprise at seeing another gentleman in the very nearly unsavory saloon, assented to Hawkes' request to have a few words with him by pointing a finger to the chair opposite him.

"Is there something I can do for you, Mr, ah, Hawkes?" asked the younger Dunmore as Hawkes placed himself in the indicated chair.

"I'm a private investigator," returned Hawkes. "Your brother–"

"A Pinkerton?" broke in Dunmore.

"No, I work alone. Your brother has requested that I look into a series of violent attacks made against him and if possible determine who is responsible."

"Attacks? What attacks? Is he all right?" The concern appeared genuine.

"Yes, he's fine. Except of course for the fact that he is frightened very nearly out of his wits. His life has been threatened twice, the last attack occurred last night. A shot was fired through his window while he sat reading. Luckily for him, the shot was wide."

"A shot? But why? Who? Wait, that's why you're here. What the devil! You think that I–" Indignation appeared in his voice.

Hawkes' gaze remained fastened upon him. "Your brother believes it possible that you are the one behind these attacks. He came to me asking that I either confirm or disprove his suspicion. Also because he has your welfare at heart. He came to me, rather than the police, as he doesn't want you to be imprisoned even if it is proven you are guilty of these attacks against him."

46

Dunmore appeared dumbfounded. "Me?–He actually believes I would shoot at him?" He shook his head and mumbled an obscenity.

"I'm here to talk with you, and perhaps in doing so gain a reason to believe that you are not responsible for these attacks."

Dunmore's eyes filled with contempt. "Now why should I care a rotten fig what you believe?"

"Do you have regard for what your brother believes?"

"My brother. A rare gem. To actually suspect me–" Once again he shook his head. "Well, ask your questions then. I've no reason not to answer them."

The waiter, a fat man with a red face and hands so plump that his knuckles were hidden beneath dimples surrounded by fat, brought Dunmore's lunch to the table. Charles picked up the glass filled with beer and took a long swallow. "Ask then I said," he demanded, as he put the glass back on the table.

"Do you know of anyone who might want to kill your brother?" inquired Simon as he watched Dunmore push his fork into a piece of potato and bring it up to his mouth.

"No, my brother is morbidly unassuming. I doubt he has an enemy in the world."

"That's bad for you. You are in need of money, I understand?"

Anger reappeared in Dunmore's face as he halted his effort to consume his meal. "You're suggesting that I would kill my brother for money." He spoke as if uttering a threat.

"Very astute of you," replied Hawkes nonchalantly.

Dunmore grunted and swallowed the piece of potato in his mouth. "Mr Hawkes. Frank is a pompous lily-livered fool, but he is my brother. I would never hurt him."

"Do you possess a Smith & Wesson?" asked Simon.

"Why–no."

"The pistol in your pocket is not a Smith & Wesson?"

"Well, you are observant, aren't you?" responded Dunmore. In a moment he produced his pistol and placed it on the table beside the plate of half-eaten cabbage and potatoes. It was a

Mauser with a hinged frame, the zig-zag grooving on the cylinder an immediate give-away as to the manufacturer.

"Thank you. May I ask, where were you last night?"

Dunmore picked up the pistol and put it away. The muscles in his jaw rippled. "I've told you I'm not responsible for any attack on my brother," he hissed.

"Last night?" insisted Hawkes.

Dunmore's nostrils flared as he inhaled and released a deep breath. "I was unfortunately alone. Recovering from the previous night which lasted until well past the morning. I had too much to drink and I'm ashamed to say spent the next night in bed, recovering. It was the one night of the week I remained in my flat."

"I see," murmured Hawkes, not convinced.

"Mr. Hawkes, I assure you I had absolutely nothing to do with these attacks. Nothing. I give you my word!"

"One of the prices one pays for choosing to live as you live is that the value of your assurances decreases proportionately. The night of the fifth, where were you then?"

Dunmore accepted the sharp chastisement without complaint.

"The fifth? Is that when the first attack occurred?"

Hawkes nodded his head and Dunmore's brow creased with thought. "No, I'm sorry," he said after a few seconds. "No, I don't recall." Then, seeing the dubious expression on Hawkes' face, he added. "That's the truth of it."

"May I ask where it is you were just coming from?" asked Hawkes.

"Before coming here? Why?"

"Please answer."

"I-I was just in my room. Getting washed and dressed."

"Alone?"

"Why–yes, as a matter of fact. Why does it matter? Has something happened?"

"No harm has come to your brother," he replied, clearly dissatisfied with the lack of verifiable information coming out of

Charles Dunmore. "You really are quite a contrast to your brother," he said, after studying the man for a few seconds. "Almost opposites, both physically and in spirit."

Dunmore chuckled. "I've sometimes thought I was a foundling, deposited on my parents' doorstep, although they always denied it."

"You need not fear they were keeping a secret from you. It's clear you and your brother are blood relations," stated Hawkes flatly.

"Oh, and how can you be so certain?"

"Your ears. I've written on the subject of the human ear more than once and more than once the knowledge has helped me resolve a case. The human ear is very unique as a rule, yet I note similarities between yours and those of your brother. These similarities would not exist if you were not related through blood."

Dunmore was impressed. "Is that so?" he remarked as his left hand went up to the side of his head and touched his ear. "The ears–amazing. I must say you are a very perceptive man." For the moment Dunmore's voice contained true admiration.

"Elementary," replied Hawkes.

"Poor Frank. We've got the same ears but little else. Too much of our father is in him. His life, our father's I mean, was as dreary as is my brother's. Life is meant to be lived."

"And that consists primarily of going to the racetrack or gambling den and consorting with less than reputable women."

"For the time being it does," agreed Dunmore readily and without a trace of shame in the smile that curled on his lips. "You've just reminded me of something, an event that occurred when I was just sixteen. Do you want to hear it?"

Hawkes replied that he did. "By all means."

"My father was continually exhorting us to 'virtue', which in his mind meant working all day and avoiding anything that even hinted at pleasure. I always chafed against his preaching, but one day it all turned to balderdash as far as I was concerned. Here's what happened. One night, a friend and I were looking for a bit of fun after having a little to drink. He had learned of a gambling house on Houston Street and we went round to it. All the time, I could hear my father's warnings in my ears. 'Never gamble. Inevitably you'll lose and destroy your life.'

"With his admonitions ringing in my ears I made my bets. To my astonishment I won. Long story short, by the end of the night I'd won the equivalent of what it would take my father six months of sweat to earn. I was elated. I felt a sense of–of power that I'd never experienced before. It was wonderful."

"Has gambling always been so kind to you?" responded Hawkes, pointing a finger at Dunmore's plate of cabbage and potatoes. "This is not a rich man's lunch nor an elegant eatery."

"No, admittedly not. But it's given me some good moments, and I'm prepared to pay for the good times by suffering through the bad. What my late father and brother could not understand is that different lives are necessary for different natures. My brother's life is–what?–a lukewarm one, neither hot nor cold. His lifestyle is proper for him but I could no sooner live his way than he could live mine. Do you understand?"

Hawkes understood very well and found himself sympathizing, at least in this one aspect, with the man. He started to rise from the table, concluding the interview, when Dunmore's words pulled him back down. "Wait a moment, I can think of someone," he declared abruptly, "someone who might want to harm my brother." Hawkes, sitting, cocked an inquisitive eye at him, a request to continue.

"A fellow named Madden," said Dunmore. "He worked as my father's accountant a few years back, before my father passed on. My father had the man arrested, at Frank's insistence if I remember correctly, when he learned Madden was embezzling funds from him. As I remember, he was sentenced to a mild prison term. Three or four years. But it ruined his life. I saw him just a few days back. Almost didn't recognize him, he was so changed. He looked terrible. I started to pass him by on the street but then he recognized me as well. He burst into a literal torrent of verbal abuse, clearly blaming the Dunmore family for his downfall. I actually was thinking about letting him suffer some retribution for his outrageous words but I guess he saw my anger was rising as he suddenly cut off and walked away from me as fast as he could. I didn't give him any further thought, until now."

"An embezzler? Why didn't your brother mention him? He was aware of the crime, was he not?"

Dunmore pursed his lips in thought and then shrugged his shoulders. "It may be he's forgotten all about the affair. It occurred, as I said, a few years back." I may not have thought of it either except I chanced to cross paths with the man. He's lucky he turned and walked away from me otherwise he would have learned that not all Dunmores are limp and alike. I would have given him the beating of his miserable life right then and there." Some heat entered Dunmore's voice with the last declaration.

"Do you have a first name for the man?"

"No–yes, Edward, I think."

"Any idea where the man is staying?"

"Not a clue."

"Thank you. I will look into it," said Hawkes, standing once again. "If you think of anything further you can contact me at The Dead Rabbit's Society. I've a room there. Good day."

Outside, as he walked from the Pigeon and Blindman's Alley, Hawkes considered the results of his interview. Inconclusive at best. He wasn't prepared to state for certain that the young man was being entirely truthful with him but neither could he say he was not. Charles Dunmore's reaction to his brother's danger appeared genuine as did his indignation at being suspected for being the cause of it. If not, the man had to be considered an actor of some talent.

Charles Dunmore had given Hawkes a name: Edward Madden. Perhaps Hawkes' contacts at the Elizabeth Street precinct could trace him. The man had to be located and investigated and, if indeed he proved to be an avenger in pursuit of what he perceived to be a personal wrong, brought forward to satisfy the demands of justice.

CHAPTER TEN

The next morning found Hawkes in a landau on his way to the purlieu of Brooklyn, specifically to a boarding house located on the other side of that magnificent achievement of modern science and engineering, the span known to the world as the Brooklyn Bridge. It was there, on the other side of the great span, that he would find Edward Madden, or at least hoped to do so, based upon the information supplied to him by Detective Hawthorne of the New York City Police Department. Hawthorne was a good man, although an alumnus of what Holmes thought of as the tenacious but uninspired school of investigation, as indeed were most individuals on police and detective forces the world over.

The sun bathed the bridge and its spider-web-like cabling in its strong glare. A hazy tenuous mist floated upon the river waters. The fresh morning sky was unblemished with clouds at the commencement of the dawn. It was still a tender new day. Only a dray and another cab were on the bridge, the horse pulling it along appearing already weary. Beside the landau Hawkes saw the bridge's two cable roads; a cable car was moving along one now, pulled by the great steam powered cable to which it was attached.

Hawkes leaned back in the seat of the cab tapping a finger and humming to himself strands of Dvorak's "New World Symphony" which he'd attended the previous night with George Hammond, Hammond soliciting him at the last moment as his wife declined to go with him due to a slight illness. During the course of the night, Hammond had reiterated to Hawkes his intention of leaving the city for his country home the next day and surprised Hawkes a bit with the information that Dunmore would be going along, the invitation that Hammond had extended to the fearful man having been, with only a slight hesitation, accepted.

Dunmore, to the dissatisfaction of Hawkes, had refused his suggestion to hire a bodyguard, just as Hawkes had feared he would.

The journey over the Brooklyn Bridge required scant minutes and the additional distance to the dilapidated building in which Edward Madden resided only a few minutes more. It was an ill-kept, aging clapboard boardinghouse standing in the midst of a row of like buildings huddled together, it appeared, to gain strength from each other so as to keep from falling down. Sitting above and on either side of the entrance, like a bandleader's epaulets, were two signs, one stating the name of the establishment and the other, the sign on the right, declaring the daily and weekly rates for obtaining a room.

Giving the driver instructions to wait, Hawkes went up the old wooden steps and entered the building. In moments he obtained the room number in which Madden was living and was knocking upon his door, the door to the last room at the very end of a rather long, narrow and foul corridor.

Getting no response, Hawkes knocked once more, louder this time. His efforts this time elicited from inside the mumbled curses of a man obviously angered over being pulled from his sleep. The voice demanded Hawkes leave him alone and, in response, the detective pounded his fist hard upon the door once more.

"Mr. Madden," he shouted. "I'd like a few words. Open the door."

The door was pulled open and before Simon stood a stocky man of average height clad in shirt and pants that hung loosely upon his frame. The clothes were badly wrinkled due to his sleeping in them and there were patches of severe wear in the stained shirt. His unshaven face was engraved with lines that gave him the impression of perpetual anger. His light brown hair was in need of a trim. He stared hard at Hawkes, his lips compressed so thin that it seemed he had no lips at all. "Why you bangin' on my door?" he demanded, his eyes taking an instant to run up and down the length of Hawkes' frame before returning again to the detective's face. "Get away!" He started to push the door closed, but Hawkes was ready, having long ago become hardened to this kind of behavior. He extended his arm and pressed a palm against the door, forcing it to remain open. Madden, realizing immediately that his strength was no match for that of the stranger in front of him, relented. "Well then," he growled. "What is it?"

"A few minutes of your time, Mr. Madden. I'd like to ask you some questions."

"My momma told me not to talk to strangers," responded Madden, hissing a laugh. "Why should I answer any questions of yours? You a copper?"

Simon shook his head. At the same time he reached into his pocket and, in the next moment, displayed before Madden's eyes a gleaming gold coin, a ten dollar gold American Liberty. The man's eyes immediately began salivating with greed at the sight of it. "I'm prepared," stated Hawkes, "to give you this coin if you will do me the kindness of answering some questions. There is only one condition to getting the money. You must speak only the truth. If I catch you misstating the facts you don't get paid."

Madden's eyes tightened on Simon as his mind calculated the chances that the offer was legitimate. Then, reaching a decision, he opened the door wide, stepped aside and allowed Hawkes to enter.

The room was nothing more than a small box with a single window. A worn and weary bed was pushed into a corner. Nearby was a washing stand. The only other furniture was a pair of wooden chairs, an old table and a marred shabby bureau. A second door, concealing a small closet, was by the bureau. A gas lamp, unlit, sat in the middle of the table. The paint was peeling from the bare walls. Poor lodgings, indeed.

"A man's home is his castle," remarked Madden, seeing Simon's gaze going about the room.

"A few years back you were employed as an accountant by the Dunmore family, is that correct?"

"It is," came the terse reply.

"You embezzled money and, as a consequence, ended by being arrested and sentenced to a prison term."

Madden emitted an angry snort. "And this is my lot because of it." He waved an arm about the room. "I can't get decent work. My life is ruined 'cause of the Dunmores." Madden fairly spit out the last word.

"You did steal from them, did you not?"

"They didn't have to deliver me over to the police. I would have paid it all back—"

"Perhaps you, having decided to steal, are now simply suffering the consequence of your own crime. If you cannot get decent work now it is because when you had a position of trust you used it to steal."

"You working for them—the Dunmores?" asked Madden with fire in his eyes.

"I'm paying to ask you the questions, remember? Do you own a Smith & Wesson .44?"

"And if I do?"

"May I see it?"

"That ain't part of the deal. You just ask questions."

"It's part of the deal if I say so. May I see it?"

Hawkes' hand went into his jacket and gripped his own revolver as, begrudgingly, Madden went to the old bureau, opened the top drawer and pulled out a pistol. "Take it out by the barrel, please," said Hawkes firmly and the man complied, lifting the pistol out of the drawer and presenting it to Hawkes who, turning his back on Madden for a few moments, stepped nearer the window into the light and checked the cylinder. "Russian cartridges," he murmured. Then, still with his back to Madden, "It's been discharged recently. One shot has been fired."

"I-I shot at a rat. Out in the back. It was sitting there looking at me so I took a crack at it. Missed it."

"You ran into Charles Dunmore recently, did you not?" asked Hawkes, continuing to check the pistol.

"I happened to spot him walking along. It made me boil just to look at him."

55

"You approached him and made threats against him," stated Hawkes, finally turning around to face Madden again.

Madden's eyebrows slid up his forehead. "Approached him, yes, but I didn't threaten him. I said a few angry words but– what's this about? Why are you here?"

"Franklin Dunmore has been the victim of an attack. A shooting attack. The attacker had a .44 Smith & Wesson." Hawkes held Madden's pistol up, holding it by the barrel.

"You trying to implicate me! Shooting? Is he dead?" Madden's face filled with fear. "It wasn't me done it! Find another patsy to pin it on! Whatever happened, it wasn't me done it! And if another Dunmore's dead so much the better for the world!"

"Would you have any objection if I took a quick look around this room, Mr. Madden?"

"You ask a lot for your gold. Look to your heart's content. If you don't mind getting your hands dirty."

"Thank you, I have no objection." Madden stood by sullenly while Hawkes made a quick and thorough search of the room. It required only a few minutes. "Helloa," he said when he opened the closet door. There a well tailored suit and a fine pair of black boots greeted his eyes. "What's this?"

"Them's my good clothes. I do my job hunting in that suit. For good jobs that is. Not that it helps. Good jobs ain't the kind I get any more. It's the only decent clothes I own."

Hawkes picked up the boots. Square-toed. Last polished perhaps a week ago, maybe a few days longer. The leather was well cared for and without the slightest bruise or sign of wear. Evidently not worn often, a sign of the dismal employment opportunities coming the way of Edward Madden.

Hawkes returned the boots to the closet floor, closed the door and placed the pledged gold coin on the table. "Good day to you, Mr. Madden," he said, handing the Smith & Wesson back to the man at last. "Thank you for your time." With that he started to stride from the room. He was halted by the dual sounds of the pistol being cocked and by Madden's threatening words.

"What's to stop me from putting a bullet in you and taking all your money, Mister? Can I ask you that question, huh?"

Hawkes turned and stared at the man, noting the gleam of evil now shining in the narrowed eyes. "So you're not above committing more crimes, are you?" pronounced Hawkes coolly.

"Your gold looks mighty good to me," replied Madden, a broad grin stretching out over his face. "I might want more of it."

"It was you then, who took that shot at Franklin Dunmore. Isn't that so?"

"No, but you've given me an idea, Mister Gold Coin. Maybe I will take the next shot at him. Now empty your pockets of all that pretty gold."

"Mr. Madden, the New York City police know I'm here. I obtained your current address from a certain Detective Hawthorne with whom I believe you are familiar. Outside my cab is waiting for me. Do you really think it is possible under those circumstances that you would escape the gallows should you choose to pull that trigger."

Uncertainty began to creep into the man's eyes. "Maybe–I'll take my chances."

Hawkes shook his head, almost sadly. "You've already taken your chances once and went to prison for it. Doesn't it strike you that you might be lethally inept in the area of crime, Mr. Madden? I would judge your chances to be poor. Perhaps this will convince you." With that, he placed his hand in the pocket of his jacket.

"Careful!" hissed Madden, holding the pistol with both hands now and keeping the barrel trained upon Hawkes' chest.

Hawkes smiled and produced a closed fist evidently holding something within it. More gold, thought Madden. Hawkes stepped nearer the table and there opened his hand, dropping the contents onto the tabletop: five bullets taken from the Smith & Wesson.

"You will need bullets for that pistol if you intend to rob me, Mr. Madden," stated Hawkes, still smiling. For a moment, Madden was rigid and unmoving with surprise, he stared at

Hawkes as though suddenly put in a trance. "W-What...?" he managed to say at last. Turning the barrel of the Smith & Wesson towards him, he studied the vacant chambers that gazed back at him. "Y-You...cunning devil..." His shoulders sagged with defeat, the colour drained from his face as his arms fell to his sides and he dropped heavily into a nearby chair. "I'm done then. Call the police," he whimpered, suddenly appearing to be close to tears.

Hawkes gazed at him and made his decision. The bullets and the gold coin he left on the table. "No, I'll not call them," he stated to the crestfallen man. "Consider this your lucky day, Mr. Madden. And forego any thoughts of criminal activity. I can offer you an almost infallible guarantee that you will not escape justice for any crimes you should commit." With that final pronouncement Hawkes turned and walked from the room. Madden, uttering a small pathetic chirrup of joyful triumph, rushed to the coin and snatched it up, gripping it tight in his fist before the door was fully shut behind the form of the departing detective.

Hawkes ordered the driver to take him back over the bridge, returning to Prince Street and the Dead Rabbits. He'd yet to have his breakfast and was suddenly famished. As he settled into the seat of the cab he eliminated any consideration of Edward Madden from his thoughts and allowed his mind to return to the memory of the previous night's concert. As the landau pulled away, he was once again humming to himself his favored bits and pieces of Dvorak's "New World Symphony", murmuring softly and melodically to the rhythm of the sound of the horse's hooves, storing grist for the mill of his improvisations on the violin.

CHAPTER ELEVEN

Sherlock Holmes has, more than once, feigned the need for his presence to be elsewhere during an investigation in order to grant himself the freedom to explore the facts of a case unimpeded, or to put a suspect at an undeserved ease over his absence. As he related his story to me, recounting to me that the obligation of his other case kept him from journeying with George Hammond and Franklin Dunmore to Black Oak, Hammond's country home, I immediately voiced my opinion that he was utilizing that same device here and broke into his narrative to say so. I asked him if the other case alluded to was in fact one of little importance and was then abandoned for the time for the sake of this one, thereby granting him the freedom to travel to Black Oak without the knowledge of Dunmore or Hammond. He corrected me at once. "No," he told me. "I indeed had another investigation of paramount importance to look into. I was doing so as a direct accommodation to the New York City Police Commissioner, who not only held a position of public importance but was also a member of a prominent family. It was an incidence of blackmail against him, and the damage to him, and his family, would have been devastating. Another story for another time, Watson. It is unlikely," he added, "even if I had gone to Black Oak at that time, that my presence would have changed what occurred there. No, I'm convinced it would not have made a difference in that regard, although I do often contemplate that it may have saved other lives. Yes, other lives might have been spared."

During the days following his client's departure to Black Oak, Hawkes found his thoughts returning now and then to the unsolved question as to who it was behind the attacks being made against Franklin Dunmore. Always Hawkes' thoughts were accompanied by a sense of frustration at being unable to proceed any further in the investigation, to unravel the mystery behind the inexplicable situation in which Dunmore found himself. Additional information was needed for him to go forward.

There existed of course the possibility that the cause for the lack of progress in this mystery resided in the reticence of Franklin Dunmore himself. Being an extremely private man, it was entirely feasible that he'd failed to tell Hawkes of his entire history, keeping to himself a private act that he feared making public out of concern for suffering the opprobrium that would result from its becoming known. If so, it may be there, in that unspoken concealment, where the answer to the problem dwelled.

If that was so, and Dunmore was not being absolutely truthful and candid with him, then he may ultimately be unable to help him. It would be better, for his own sake, if Dunmore was absolutely forthcoming.

There were other moments when, in contemplation of the relatively lonely countryside which surrounded Hammond's country home, Hawkes experienced a vague uneasiness, a disquietude that he ultimately brushed aside as a valueless sensation. Nonetheless, in retrospect, he would subsequently come to believe that this foreboding on his part may indeed have presaged the event, the violent homicide, which would very shortly become known to him.

Six days had transpired since George Hammond and guests had departed for their bucolic hiatus from the, at times, jarring activities of the bustling city. In Franklin Dunmore's case, there was of course the added comfort of believing he'd succeeded in placing some distance between him and the clandestine phantom pursuing him. That he had succeeded, with that distance, for a time at least, in escaping the threat of further villainy against him. In that optimistic belief he was soon proven dreadfully mistaken.

Heavy rain had fallen during the day, a drenching storm that served to cleanse the streets of the city. Many of the roadways, near the kerbs, were for a time transformed into rushing rivulets in which floated the shunned detritus of the city, all flowing into newly formed small lakes. By nightfall however, the storm had moved on, the sky had cleared and much of the rainwater had drained from the streets, leaving behind a sparkling coat of sleek wetness and bringing a pleasant, fresh, cool taste to the city air. Simon carried with him, as he returned to The Dead Rabbits Society, the satisfaction of the pleasant night and the anticipation, equally satisfying, of a possible breakthrough in "The Case of the Wayward Police Commissioner". There was more to be done, that was certain, but Hawkes had every hope of solving the case shortly. This satisfaction immediately began to dissipate when, upon arriving at his destination, the desk clerk handed him a telegram that had been held and waiting for him. Ripping open the sealed envelope and reading the message it contained, he discovered his worse fears to be validated. Murder had occurred at Black Oak.

Another attempt had been made against the life of Franklin Dunmore and, while that hunted man had once more been fortunate enough to escape harm, another had not been so favored by chance: Amelia Hammond, George Hammond's young and beautiful wife, had been shot dead, a victim of the errant bullet aimed at Dunmore.

Hawkes had no choice but to present himself in person at Black Oak immediately, the crisis there demanded it. His attention to the predicament of the Police Commissioner, however close to resolution it was, would have to be trusted to the police detectives assisting him in the case.

CHAPTER TWELVE

Hawkes was riding the rails of the Ulster & Delaware Railroad by nine A.M. the following morning, his destination the Grand Hotel Station forty miles or so past the Kingston Junction. There he'd have to find transportation to Hammond's house, Black Oak. That should not present a problem, reasoned Hawkes, since the Grand Hotel, the "New Grand", was a popular resort servicing a booming tourist trade composed of a rather high class clientele. There should be no difficulty in obtaining a carriage there. Hammond's own home was just a few miles distance from it.

It was a scenic ride, offering Hawkes dramatic picturesque mountain views. While it was his first time aboard the Ulster & Delaware, Hawkes was not surprised to be greeted by the mountains, not after viewing the three hissing Ten-Wheelers that were used to pull the eight-car passenger train he boarded. That much pulling power spoke of the need to conquer steep grades. He was however struck by the unexpected and extraordinary natural beauty of the soaring countryside through which he passed. Much of it undisturbed forest, still held in the hands of the Almighty.

It was not long out of Kingston that Hawkes was standing on the Grand Hotel Station. His first sight of the hotel impressed him. It was more than worthy of its name. A large building of Victorian design, over an eighth of a mile in length with a mansard roof and four towers. Services were provided by the hotel in abundance and Hawkes found it an easy matter to obtain a wagonette to carry him the rest of the way to Black Oak. It was near noontime that he'd arrived at Hammond's country home.

The house known as Black Oak possessed its own singular history, one which Hawkes would shortly come to learn the facts of in conversations with Hammond and his servants. It was a chronicle that was, in its own way, as sensational as that of the legend of the curse of Baskerville Hall although, having stated that, I must hastily add that the record of violence at Black Oak, and the local superstitions it gave rise to, played no part in the murder that occurred there, despite the opinions voiced by some who thought otherwise at the time. The house was named for the century-old great gnarled oak tree standing before it. Blistered and twisted by the volition of Nature, its trunk had obtained an image upon it of a man, a screaming terrified man, who appeared to have been ensnared and absorbed into the bark while still alive, to be entombed, screaming for release, within the immense five-foot diameter of the trunk of the tree.

The dwelling was composed of various sized pieces of grey sombre stone and faced the great oak with a silent scowl. The house had been erected more than seventy years earlier by a gentleman named Alexander Wilks, a man renowned in his youth for feats of bravery during the War of 1812, that armed conflict which settled forever the question between the colonies and the Empire as to which would rule the New World.

By 1820 Wilks had attained a fortune through trade and, becoming engaged to be married, had the house built for his use and that of his new bride.

The blushing maiden no doubt entered into matrimony believing she would be happy in love. Unfortunately, this was not to be and she soon discovered happiness to be a poor lost soul wandering far from her home and locked outside its doors, forbidden entry into Black Oak. Wilks' expressions of love for her were very shortly offered in sharp blows and violent words. The bride endured her husband's ill treatment for a terrible six years at the end of which, in a fit of fury, Mr. Wilks ended her suffering by plunging a knife blade deep into his wife's chest, killing her. She lived just long enough, so say the gossips, to curse the man before taking her last breath.

Alexander Wilks, war hero and successful entrepreneur, was now a base assassin. To hide his heinous crime from the world and, more importantly in his view, from justice, he carried the body of his wife down the steps into the cellar of Black Oak, dug out a shallow grave and placed the corpse into it. To explain his wife's sudden disappearance, he concocted a tale, telling those who inquired after her that she'd run off with another man, a drummer, American slang for a traveling salesman. The explanation contained a hint of validity since many in the area were aware of the coarse manner in which the woman was being treated by the husband. She certainly had no reason to stay. Wilks, through his concealment of his wife's body and his creation of his small fiction, had succeeded in getting away with murder.

Or had he?

For there does occur at times other means for justice to be achieved in those instances when the faulty eyes and hands of society fail to strive to attain it. Shortly thereafter the murderer began to complain, to those who would listen, of hearing noises in the dark hours of the night, groans and drones of unexplained origin that sent shivers of cold fright deep into his heart. He began to fear, and to believe, that he was now being haunted by the spirit of his own slaughtered wife. There were times, in the black hours of the night, that his screams of terror could be heard by his servants. For months the man suffered and slowly he wasted away, deteriorating physically until his skin hung loosely off his now gaunt form. His colour, formerly so healthy, became a waxy grey and his eyes, his terror-filled eyes, glittered wildly and widened in fear at every slight sound. Finally his emaciated body was discovered one stormy night, laying on the floor of his bedroom with a revolver beside it, a bullet through his heart. His murdered wife's corpse was discovered in the cellar shortly thereafter.

Superstition descended upon the house. People talked of the rumour that the spirit of Wilks' wife, so cruelly murdered, wandered the floors of the dwelling, still seeking vengeance against her husband and killer, unaware that her desire had been thwarted by Wilks own suicide, if suicide it was. Others were emphatic that it was his wife killed the evil man, that she ultimately had achieved her revenge.

The "Black" in Black Oak came then to have a double meaning, referring to the history of the house as well as to the dark hue of the trunk of the tree. The life-like figure of the screaming man suggested to some the soul of Alexander Wilks, the murderer's spirit trapped there to gaze forever at the house in which he created so much misery.

This was the house purchased by Amelia Hammond's father, George Hammond's father-in-law, and presented to the groom and bride on the day of their marriage, six years earlier, as a wedding present. Those locals who were aware of the history of the house, upon learning of the slaying of Amelia Hammond, were quick to jump to the conclusion that it was the curse of the house that had claimed her, that her father had as much to do with her death, through his purchase of the property, as the man who'd pulled the trigger of the gun that had killed her.

In response to Hawkes' knock, the door was opened by Hammond's elderly butler, William Huxley. He moved aside to allow Simon to enter and then, as the detective stepped over the threshold, closed the door behind him. "We were expecting you, sir," he said. "The Master had me send the wire."

Hawkes glanced around the house. A dismal atmosphere of tragedy seemed to pervade everything within. The nearby mirror was draped in the black crepe of loss. The butler's eyes were red-rimmed, evidence of his personal sorrow. He apparently cared deeply for Amelia Hammond.

"How is Mr. Hammond faring," inquired Hawkes.

"He's upstairs, sir," replied Huxley. "Just beginning to stir. The physician prescribed laudanum for him to help him sleep at night. Under doctor's orders he's been confined to his bed. He hasn't been out of his room since—for two days. I've never seen anyone so racked. He blames himself, you see, for inviting Mr. Dunmore to the house. It seems that he, Mr. Dunmore, was the intended victim. The shot was actually meant for him. Terrible, sir. Terrible."

"The shooting occurred two days ago?" asked Hawkes.

"Three now. When the evening comes."

65

Hawkes grunted, a bit piqued that it took so long to contact him. Much evidence can be lost due to delay. "Is it possible for me to see Mr. Hammond?"

"In an hour or so, sir. In the meantime, I'm sure the master would not consider it inappropriate for me to offer you some brandy after your trip. Would you like a glass?"

Hawkes replied that he would and the two men passed into a small drawing room, adjoining the dining room. Huxley went to the liquor cabinet from which he extracted a crystal decanter and a glass and, while the man was busy pouring the brandy into the glass, Simon went to the window. Pushing aside the rose-patterned curtains, he gazed out to the garden beyond. "It was her garden," said Huxley as he brought the brandy over. "She cultivated the plants and flowers while here. She told me once that she enjoyed the feel of the earth between her fingers. Like holding life in your hands, she said." A tear began to glisten in the corner of his right eye. "Just a week since her birthday. The master gave her that sundial you see in the middle of the garden as a present. Just a week ago he threw a surprise party for her and now–"

Hawkes, glass in hand, seated himself in a nearby armchair and pointed to another across from it. "Mr. Huxley, please sit down," he said, "and tell me exactly what you know of this tragedy. What were the exact events surrounding Mrs. Hammond's murder?"

Huxley did as requested, placing himself into the chair opposite Simon. "Poor sweet woman. It's hard to believe she's gone. I didn't see much actually. Dinner had only just been finished. I was in the butler's pantry when I heard the shot. Like an explosion, it was. I came running back to the dining room. People were shouting wildly. Who could blame them? There she was, poor thing, slumped over the table, blood all over. The shot came from the garden, and that's where some were looking and pointing, through the French Doors that open onto the garden patio."

"Did anyone go into the garden?"

"Not immediately. Even when I got there everyone seemed to be still frozen, either screaming or stunned by what'd happened. I too stopped dead in my tracks–horrible–" Huxley shook his head and this time a tear succeeded in escaping his eye to roll down his cheek. "It was Braxton," he continued without prompting, "who finally went out to the garden. I remember he'd been in the carriage-house and came running into the room as I'd done. He understood at once what had taken place, took out his pistol and went straight through the French Doors to make a search of the garden. He saw no one."

"Mr. Braxton must be a man of action," responded Hawkes. "He saw nothing unusual?"

"Not that I'm aware of. I believe that's what he told the police, that he saw nothing."

"You said Braxton was in the carriage-house. Was anyone else out of the room at the time?"

"Well, when I came into the room, I believe everyone else was there, but some had just arrived as I'd done. Mr. Hammond had gone upstairs after finishing his meal, to fetch himself a cigar. It's his habit to have a cigar or two after dinner and he'd found he'd left his smokes in his room. Two of the guests, Doctor Rogers and a young man, Robert Costes, a lawyer in Mr. Hammond's firm, were also out of the room at the time the shot was fired."

"I see," murmured Hawkes. "Pray continue."

"I remember Mr. Costes had decided against dessert and excused himself. I saw him go into the library and take a book off the shelf. I assumed he was going to his room to read. He's young, a quiet sort, wears those round gold-framed glasses. He seemed to be a bit uncomfortable in the midst of the others who were, after all, to him nothing more than strangers. I believe the only person in the room he was acquainted with, before coming to Black Oak, was Mr. Hammond."

"And Doctor Rogers? He was absent as well. Why was he out of the room?"

"I don't know," replied Huxley.

"You're certain no one else was absent at the time of the shooting?"

"Let's see, the Willis couple, they were there. They were standing off to one side when I entered. She was clinging to him as tightly as she could. Mr. Dunmore was there, his face as white as chalk. He'd been seated right beside Mrs. Hammond and I'm told the bullet missed him by no more than a hair. He appeared terribly shaken, just sitting in his chair and staring at the blood that'd splashed upon the sleeve of his jacket."

"The Willis couple. Who are they?"

"Friends of Mrs. Hammond. They were invited to Black Oak by her."

"What else do you know about them?"

Huxley shrugged his weary shoulders. "Nothing really. Oh, I do know that Mrs. Willis has very deep feelings about the movement to emancipate women. I recall she very nearly bit the doctor's head off when he made a casual remark about the foolishness of permitting women the vote."

"Does that account for everyone? Any other guests?"

"No, that's the lot."

"What about the servants? You said Braxton was in the carriage-house. You were in the pantry. Where was the cook? Are there any other servants present?"

"Charlotte's the cook, of course. She came into the room right after I did. Poor dear. Her heart is broken. When the mistress was born it was Charlotte who was hired to be the nursery maid. She feels as though, almost, that it was her own child killed. But she's a tough old soldier, God bless her. She's of the kind that keep their suffering inside. She was right back at her duties, cooking, the next day. I suppose it helps her to stay busy too. I-I hear her crying–at times." Huxley shook his head forlornly. "For the world's more full of weeping than you can understand–"

"What?"

"Oh, it's a line from a young poet, Yeats is his name," answered Huxley. "It just came to me." The servant fell silent again, turning away from Hawkes and staring, as though dazed, at the floor in front of him.

"Anyone else? Any other servants?"

"No, that's everyone," responded Huxley, blinking his eyes as though surprised to find that Hawkes was still present. "The maid did not come to Black Oak."

"Who was it summoned the police? How long was it after the murder that they arrived?"

"About an hour, I'd say. Braxton rode out for them. Being in charge of the house I'm somewhat ashamed to say that it was Braxton and Doctor Rogers who took control of the situation. I-I just stood there. Braxton, as I said, ran to the garden to search for the shooter. The doctor went to Mrs. Hammond and examined her. He had to pull poor Mr. Hammond away from her. He was leaning over her, crying like a baby, begging God not to let her die. It was terrible. I knew–I knew she was gone by the expression that came into the doctor's face. When Braxton returned from the garden the doctor asked him to ride for the police and–and to get the coroner's physician."

"And it was approximately an hour before they arrived?"

"That's right. During that time, the doctor administered laudanum to Mr. Hammond. He had to be assisted up to his room. The police, when they arrived, took statements from everyone. They had the courtesy to leave Mr. Hammond alone, thank God."

"One final question. Did you see anything or anyone unusual the day of the shooting. Anyone near the house other than the guests and staff?"

"No one," replied Huxley, with another shake of his head.

"Thank you, you've explained it all very well. I'd like to speak to everyone, starting with Braxton. Is he about?"

"Why yes, I believe he's in his room right now. I'll summon him for you. But I must tell you that most of the guests have left. Yesterday morning. The Willis couple, Doctor Rogers and young Mr. Costes. They returned to the city. Only Mr. Dunmore remains."

Hawkes grunted once more. "You have their addresses of course. I'd appreciate it if you give them to me. I'll speak now to those who remain. Would you call Braxton in please?"

"Yes, sir." With that, the elderly man rose slowly from the chair, straightened himself and left the room. Hawkes watched the servant's departing form until he was gone and then himself stood and stepped to the window, looking again at the garden formerly tended by Amelia Hammond. Another attempt upon Dunmore's life, he reflected. This time the errant bullet had not traveled harmlessly into a wall but had struck an innocent woman. A true tragedy. The garden, showing the effects of the ending of the Autumn season, seemed to be as affected by that tragedy as the members of the house, as though understanding dissolution and death and in some way aware that the woman who'd tended it had been taken from it forever.

It was a minute or two before Braxton strode into the room, Huxley by his side, escorting him. He was a large man of about forty, with very thick wide shoulders upon which sat a wide neck and a broad-featured head. Two flinty eyes peered out at Hawkes from beneath scowling brows of old scar-tissue. His brown hair was closely cut to the skull and spotted here and there with grey. Hawkes turned from the window and extended his hand as the large man came up to him. "Mr. Braxton, I assume," he said. "I'm Simon Hawkes." Huxley, his responsibility concluded, left the room.

"Pleased to meet you, sir," responded Braxton, the rough features of his face relaxing just a bit before Hawkes' friendly manner as he accepted Hawkes' proffered hand.

"Do you have a few moments? I'd like to talk to you about what happened."

A cautiousness crept into Braxton's eyes. "Talk?"

"A few questions. I understand you were in the carriage-house when you heard the shot that killed Mrs. Hammond?"

"Not entirely true. I'd just left the carriage-house. I was returning into the house. I heard the shot just outside the side entrance. The screams came right after. That's when I realized

70

something was wrong. Those screams were full of horror, you see. It raised the hairs on my neck to hear them."

"Then you came immediately to the dining room?"

"As fast as I could run."

"You carry a pistol?"

Braxton replied with a pat of his hand onto the side of his jacket. "Carry one with me. Done so for years."

"May I see it?"

Braxton, after a brief hesitation, produced and presented to Hawkes the pistol, reaching in and taking it from his pocket. A Smith & Wesson .44 with Russian cartridges in the chambers. An automatic ejection pistol.

"This has been fired very recently," he remarked as he examined it. "Two bullets are missing."

"It's my habit to do some target shooting every day or so. Keeps the eye sharp."

"I'm surprised you carry such a weapon," said Hawkes. "I understand you're an ex-pugilist and you still appear to be a man very capable of defending himself without resorting to a pistol." He punctuated his words by handing the Smith & Wesson back to Braxton, who put it away as pride suffused his features over Simon's words. Even the scar tissue above the eyes began to radiate satisfaction over the compliment.

"Yes sir. It was a time back, it was, but in my prime I fought the best. Even John L. himself. There was a fighter for you. Yes, I can take care of myself if need be. But that's also why I need the weapon. When someone tries to come against me, they at times resort to something other than fists, you see, believing I'd have the best of them in that department."

Simon accepted the common sense of Braxton's words with a sharp, quick nod of the head and Braxton, feeling he'd been granted permission to discuss his pugilist days, went on, becoming loquacious regarding a history of which he was still proud. "The heavyweight championship was won last year by that Corbett fellow but let me tell you he beat Sullivan only because they were wearing gloves. If Sullivan had his bare knuckles he'd of made mincemeat of him. Yes, I fought some good ones in my day but that John L., he could dish it out better than anyone, and take it back in return. A jaw like a rock. When I fought him there were no gloves. We fought bare-knuckled. Men fighting like men. I went twenty-five rounds with him, the last two with broken ribs, before throwing in the sponge. After the fight, he came round and shook my hand. Getting that handshake, that was a splendid moment, even though I'd lost."

"He must have thought you were good yourself," said Hawkes. "An admirable opponent."

"I was young and thought I was the toughest thing alive. Until I ran against Sullivan." Braxton shook his head and smiled, enjoying the memory. "Good ol' John L. I thought I was a hard nut but he was harder. You're right, not too many men in the world got a handshake of respect from the likes of him."

"Nor too many willing to pay the price to earn it."

"Braxton's smile beamed. "Thank you, Mr. Hawkes. You're right. Not too many."

"Mr. Braxton, you say you were, that night, outside when you heard the shot. That was followed by screams, is that correct?"

"Yes, it is. When I heard the screams I came inside."

"Quite so. So you came inside. And when you entered the dining room, what did you see?"

Braxton's mouth tightened. "God it was bad. The missus' head was on the table, red blood on the tablecloth. People screaming…"

"You went straight into the garden?"

"Right. When I saw what happened, I knew the shot came from there. It was a dark night. There was no moon to help me see, but, coming back from the outside as I was, I had my lantern with me."

"That was a brave thing to do. It was a great risk."

Braxton gave Hawkes a self-deprecating smile. "More foolish than brave, now I think on it."

"What did you see?"

"Not a blessed thing. Except for my lantern, it was black as pitch. I didn't hear or see a thing and after a few minutes of looking about I came back to the house. I saw Mr. Hammond then crying over the missus' body. There was nothing to be done—not for her. God rest her soul."

"It was you rode for the police."

"That's so. Six miles. It was a rough ride. It being so dark that night. The horse nearly stumbled once or twice."

"Yes, again you took a risk. You seem very able. Mr. Hammond is quite fortunate to have an employee such as yourself."

"Thank you, Mr. Hawkes," responded an appreciative Braxton. "That's very kind of you."

"One last question. Did you see anyone that day. A stranger? Near or about the house? Anyone who didn't belong?"

"No, no one—" Here the man paused a moment and then raised his eyebrows as a recollection came to him. "Wait a moment, yes I did," he added hastily. "Yes, it slipped my mind. There was a tramp here that afternoon. It was only for a few seconds that I spoke to him. He was looking for a handout and I shooed him on his way. There's a whole camp of gipsies, beggars, a mile or two from here. Give to one and they'd all be here, camping outside the door."

"Is that so? What did he look like?"

"A beggar. Dirty, ragged fellow. Oh, about your height I'd say. About thirty years old. He certainly looked young enough and strong enough to be working for a living. He was a bit of a snorter too. Had the gall to show me some temper when I told him to be on his way."

"Was there anything unique about him? Any distinguishing marks? A scar, for example?"

"No, no, Mr. Hawkes. Nothing I can recall at least."

At that moment Huxley entered the room and advised Hawkes that his employer was able to see him. It took Hawkes a moment to thank Braxton for his time and then he and the manservant went together out of the room.

"How is he?" queried Hawkes as the two men strode the hall towards Hammond's room.

"He appears–worse to me," replied Huxley grimly. "He's taking it hard. He and the missus–were quite close." The butler's voice trailed off and he offered a sad shake of his head as the termination of the sentence.

George lay on the bed, his upper body propped up with pillows, a light blue blanket covering him from the chest down, dressed in his pajamas beneath a long silk robe. The room was left dark, and it was not until after Huxley left and Hawkes stepped closer to the invalid that he could discern his features. He was very pale, even sickly. His eyes glistened as though with fever, the whites surrounding the irises were speckled with red.

"Helloa, Simon," he spoke up wearily. "It's good of you to respond so quickly to my wire."

"How are you faring?" asked Hawkes.

Hammond waved the inquiry away. "What does it matter?" In the next instant the man's composure broke. "She's gone, gone–" A sob escaped him and his face wrenched with pain just before it fell into his hands. Hawkes waited the few moments it took for the man to exercise his will and compose himself once more. "Excuse me," murmured Hammond, lifting his head to look at Hawkes once again. "I'm sorry. Excuse me."

"Are you up to–"

"Oh, I can't live without her!" groaned Hammond in a choking voice, rocking to and fro against the pillows and closing his eyes. "I-I can't!" Here was a man in bad shape indeed, very close to brain fever. Huxley was right to fear for him. "Oh God, it's my fault! My fault! If I hadn't invited Dunmore here, this wouldn't have happened! Oh God! She's dead because of me!"

Hawkes didn't immediately discredit the statement, struck both by the partial truth of the words as well as by the enormous guilt that was evidently crushing the man. Finally, placing a compassionate hand on the man's shoulder, he said softly. "Calm yourself. The only one truly to blame is the man who pulled the trigger."

Hammond ceased his rocking and stared at Hawkes, the muscles in his jaw clenching and unclenching as though physically digesting his words. "Will you catch him, Simon? Will you catch the fiend who killed my wife?" There was anger in him now. "You must! You must! And when you do you must tell me who it is!" His voice was growing fierce with heat. "You mustn't go to the police. You must give him to me! You must give him to me."

"What? What are you saying?"

"I want to kill the monster myself! Myself! When you find him tell me who it is so I can kill him! You must do that! You must!"

Hawkes was startled by the man's vehemence. "It's your grief talking," he replied at last. "You–"

"I want Amelia's killer to die by my hands! My hands!" hissed Hammond, forgetting his exhaustion and holding his hands up as though they were clutching an unseen throat. In the next moment, all rage and energy left him and, his weary body having expended most of the feeble resources it was then capable of, he sank back upon his pillows, his hands going up to his face again. "Oh God, my poor, poor Amelia," he moaned into his palms, closing his eyes tightly. "My dear sweet wife–"

"Perhaps it would be better if I left. We can–"

"No, don't go," objected Hammond, his voice little more than a whisper now. "Please ask your questions. If I can–tell you something–anything–that will assist you in catching this fiend, let me do so."

"Very well. Just a few questions. I have the primary facts from the others so I'll be brief. During the course of dinner everyone was at the table, is that correct?"

"Yes, we were all there."

"Afterwards, tea was offered to the guests?"

"Tea and coffee. Desserts."

"Who are the guests who declined it?"

"Declined it? Who? Dr. Rogers and my clerk, Bob Costes. They both excused themselves from the table. I remember because I left at the same time. I discovered I'd neglected to take my cigars downstairs with me. I returned to fetch them."

"How long have you known them? The doctor and Mr. Costes?"

"Rogers has been my physician since my marriage. He was my wife's doctor first. Costes is a clerk in my law office. A hard worker. Had him only a short time, a few weeks now."

"The Willis couple. How long have you known them?"

"I-I don't. That is, Amelia is friendly with them. Was–for a few years I suppose."

"Did you take notice of where either man went after they left the dining room?"

"No, I didn't pay any attention."

"Your servants, are you aware of where they were at the time?"

"No, I mean, not exactly. Huxley and Charlotte were busy with the coffee and tea. Braxton, I don't know what he was doing."

"Have you seen anyone unusual, a stranger, on your property recently?"

"No. No one."

"Where were you when you heard the shot?"

"I-I was in here, our–this room. My heart stopped when I heard it. I-I remember thinking, my God, Dunmore's been shot. I-I went running down the stairs and when I saw Dunmore, alive, I was actually relieved." Hammond laughed, an unnatural low laugh. "I was relieved to see him alive." The peculiar laugh began again and then transformed into sobbing as Hammond brought his hands up slowly to his face. "Then, I saw–my Amy." His shoulders shook with his sobs. The man appeared to be close to a total collapse.

"This is difficult for you," said Simon. "I'll be going now. You should get back to your rest."

Hammond gazed sorrowfully at him. "I-I wish now the bullet had not missed him," he declared, weakly, speaking of Dunmore. "That it was he who was dead now. I-I–"

76

"I will do my best to put my hand on the man who did this," stated Hawkes solemnly. "You have my word on that." His face was grave as the two men gazed at each other for a few moments. At last, Hammond responded in his fatigued voice, "Thank you. Remember, remember what I said," he added, his voice a whisper now, "You tell me first. You tell me–who it is." Hawkes turned away, saying nothing, as the weary invalid closed his eyes.

Huxley was in the hall when Hawkes emerged from Hammond's room. "The doctor was of the opinion he should be moved to a hospital," whispered the butler to Hawkes as though imparting a secret. "But Mr. Hammond wouldn't agree. The missus, her body, will go back to the city tonight and he insists upon accompanying her on the train. We're scheduled to return tomorrow and she'll be buried the day after. Perhaps he'll be a bit stronger by then. I really don't see how he'll be able to attend the funeral otherwise, in the shape he's in."

"It will be an effort, that's certain. I wonder if I could make one further imposition upon you," said Hawkes. "I would be obliged if you would direct me to the dining room in which Mrs. Hammond was killed."

All evidence of the shocking crime was gone, the table had been cleared, the room cleaned. Hawkes, alone now having dismissed Huxley, walked around the dinner table, circling it, his face set, looking like a beast of prey closing in upon an unseen quarry known to it only by the slightest scent rising on the wind.

George Hammond was sitting here, he told himself as he touched the top of the back of one of the chairs, his wife here. Next to her Franklin Dunmore. The seating arrangement of the guests had been given to Hawkes by the butler before the manservant left the room.

Yes, there was a spot of blood where Amelia Hammond had been sitting, left behind on the table despite the efforts of the staff to clean up. After a few moments Hawkes went to the French Doors and opened them. The twittering of birds came sweeping into the room, carried inside by the fragrant breeze coming off the garden. The doors opened onto a small patio which, in turn, led to the garden beyond. The garden was enclosed on three sides by a tall red-brick wall that provided privacy and a sense of solitude from the countryside beyond. The wall of the house, broken by the French Doors, completed the enclosure on the fourth side. A narrow path of flagstone meandered from the patio to a few feet before an iron gate in the brick wall opposite the house. The gate was approximately four feet in height.

In the centre of the garden was the gleaming brass sundial, Amelia's birthday present. It was large, fully three feet in diameter, a disk of bright brass that lay on the ground. Nearby were a few wrought-iron benches, rusted in spots, evidently here in the garden for years.

Hawkes studied the ground by the patio. Something, pressed into the earth, sparkled up the sunlight to his eyes and, bending over, he worked it free. A .44 Russian cartridge. Someone's foot had pressed it into the ground. Braxton, or perhaps the police. He placed it into his pocket.

Simon walked slowly along the path to the gate. A large bush leaned against the wall beside the gate. He saw the moist and soft earth, the grass and flowers here, trampled and crushed down by the police. "Like a herd of buffalo," he muttered to himself, giving voice, not for the first time, to his opinion of the manner in which the police, much too often and through their own carelessness, obliterate evidence that might exist at the scene of a crime.

He turned his attention to the gate itself. He tried to open it but could not. It remained stubbornly closed. The hinges were rusted absolutely shut. It led to a small narrow dirt road on the other side, a trail leading away from the garden and the house. The earth was full of tracks. The police again, assessed Hawkes. There were no deep depressions in the trail's soft earth, a fact which caused Hawkes to frown with concentration and thought.

In the brick of the wall, near the garden gate, was a patch of brick that was recently repaired. Very close to this repair stood a garden shed. Opening its door, Hawkes saw an array of gardening tools and a wooden board on which someone had recently mixed cement. Next to the board was a trowel, also showing signs of recent use.

Simon closed the shed door and returned his gaze to the wrought-iron gate. Then he let his eyes survey the garden grounds. The brick wall was concealed from view in many places by the trees, plants and hedges that grew against it. Staying close to the wall, Simon walked the garden's perimeter until he spied a narrow half-overgrown path paved with brick hidden behind some tall hedges. "Helloa," he said as he spied what he was searching for, another door, another way in and out of the garden.

A small door, no taller in height than he was, painted green, the paint peeling away in spots exposing the bare wood underneath. Simon turned the handle and it opened easily. On the other side of the door was another row of thick hedges which served to conceal the door from that side as well.

But there was sufficient space between those hedges and the wall for someone to squeeze by, and, Hawkes saw immediately, someone had recently done exactly that. A broken twig at shoulder height and footprints in the earth offered ample evidence of that. The local police had not been here, that too was clear. They had not discovered the second door.

He followed the footprints a few feet until a thinning in the hedge permitted him to pass through without effort, stepping to a clay and gravel path that ran parallel with the hedges until it turned at the end of the garden wall to run along the side of the house. Here and there, on this side of the house, a flower pot decorated the edge of the path, a spot of colour against the dull brown of the earth.

Simon followed the footpath until he came to a side door of the house. The door Braxton used to enter after leaving the carriage-house. Twisting the handle he discovered the door to be locked. The sunlight reflected off the lone pane of glass in the door and Hawkes had to press close to the glass and raise his hands to block the sun in order to achieve a view of the interior beyond the door. He saw a narrow hall.

He stood in contemplation for a few minutes before retracing his steps up the gravel path, returning through the green door into the garden and finally into the dining room of Black Oak.

CHAPTER THIRTEEN

"Good day, Charlotte," said Huxley to the woman's back as he and Hawkes entered the kitchen. Her spine went rigid at the sound of the manservant's voice. She was seated at a small oval table in a corner, peeling a modest mound of potatoes sitting in front of her and had to twist round in her chair to face the two men now standing behind her. "This is Mr. Simon Hawkes," introduced Huxley. "He's here at the Master's request. He has a few questions for you." With that pronouncement, and responding to a cue from Hawkes, the servant left the room.

Charlotte's distress was clearly evidenced by her dark, sunken, sorrow-filled eyes. Tears glittered now at the crests of her full cheeks. "Yes, sir. How do you do, sir?" she said, putting down the small knife with which she was peeling the potatoes and casting her eyes up to Hawkes' face.

She'd been Amelia's nursery maid years earlier, prior to becoming the family cook. A plump, large bosomed woman of fifty years of age with straight black hair, streaked with grey, which was pulled back with a fierce severity from her forehead. Her pale blue eyes, if they had not been filled with grief as they were, would have radiated gentleness. Over the black of the dress she wore was a tan well-used apron.

"Well, thank you," said Hawkes, taking a place at the table. "How are you faring?" he asked, gazing into the plump woman's face. There was tenderness in Hawkes' voice and his gentle inquiry caused the collapse of Charlotte's stoic containment of her sorrow. With Simon's polite question, her composure shattered like brittle glass and she burst into tears, bringing her hands up to her face and sobbing into the palms. "Oh sir—my poor lady—" Sobs shook her stout body. "My poor baby—I held her in—in my arms—when she was a babe—a little ball of fat she was. I took care of her, watched her grow—" Her sobs increased so that she was incapable of speaking further and the woman

81

lowered her face to her hands a second time, giving herself over to her sorrow. Hawkes comforted her as best he could, patting her shoulder and speaking to her in his soothing way which he could employ when necessary. He waited. It was a minute or so before she recovered sufficiently to be able to bring her emotions under control. Using a corner of her apron she wiped her moist cheeks and wet eyes. "I must get back to work," she murmured into the cloth of her apron.

A strong woman, concluded Hawkes. "Charlotte, if you're up to it, I would like to ask you a few questions about that night."

She gazed into his face for a time before nodding her head. "Very well," she told him, squaring her shoulders.

In a narrative broken intermittently with tears, the sorrowful woman told him her account of the events surrounding the slaying of her beloved mistress. It differed in no substantive way from the facts as related to him by Huxley and Braxton.

The distress filling the house was matched by that suffered by Franklin Dunmore although the underlying cause of distress was clearly not the same. In the others the cause was sorrow and grief, in Dunmore's, it was pure unadulterated fear.

Hawkes was shown to Dunmore's room by Huxley immediately after leaving the grieving cook in the kitchen. Dunmore was clad in a light flannel robe and wearing red slippers on his feet, the colour of which contrasted with the pale white, blue-veined skin there. He was thinner now than previously, his face heavy and haggard. His harassed eyes, ringed with purple, stared at Simon with a timorous uncertainty. The skin of his face was waxy and the normally fastidious man had shaved poorly. He failed to extend his hand to Hawkes, offering Simon only a quick perfunctory nod of the head as the detective came into the room.

"How are you?" asked Hawkes as he and Dunmore placed themselves into facing armchairs. In response the small man held out his right hand to exhibit the trembling he was unable to bring under control. "That's how I am, Mr. Hawkes. Scared to death."

A pitiable tone dominated his voice. He looked as though he might burst into tears at any moment just as Charlotte had done. "I-It is this–this living under constant fear. I'm afraid of everything. It is more than flesh and blood can bear! If-If not for the sedative Doctor Rogers has given me, I-I believe I would go out of my mind entirely."

"Are you able to discuss the details of what happened?"

Dunmore pressed a hand to his temple and shut his eyes. It was a moment before he responded. "Forgive me, I-I feel dizzy at times. It was ghastly. One moment Mrs. Hammond was sitting there–beside me, smiling and chatting in that friendly way of hers, and–and the next–my God–"

Hawkes waited a few moments before requesting Dunmore to go on.

"Suddenly there was an–explosion," continued the terrified man, clearly reliving the events now in his mind, his eyes looking down at his own lap. "An explosion from the other side of the French Doors and the side of her head turned–crimson. God in heaven, it was horrible! An instant later and her head crashed onto the table. Not just falling down but rather as though an invisible hand had pushed her head down from the back. Oh, there was blood! Blood everywhere! Some splashed on me. On my hand–" Dunmore raised his hand and studied it as though examining it for remaining stains. He attempted to say more but his voice faded into sobs. It was a time before he spoke again. When he did, it was through clenched teeth, as though he was experiencing physical pain. "Oh God, why is this happening? Why does someone want to kill me?" He fastened his eyes upon Simon's face. "Please, you've got to discover who's doing this. It's destroying me! I'm literally going out of my mind!" With a gesture of despair punctuating his words he turned his face away. Here was a man, thought Hawkes, worse off than even Hammond. He waited a minute until he felt Dunmore had regained some of his composure before speaking.

"Mr. Dunmore," he said, speaking in the same kindly tones he'd used with Charlotte. "May I continue?"

The small man nodded his head.

"What did you do when you realized that Mrs. Hammond had been shot?"

"D-Do?" Dunmore seemed confused by the question.

"Did you continue to sit? Did you reach for her? What was your immediate reaction?"

"I-I'm ashamed to say, it was not one of bravery. I just sat there, staring, in disbelief, and then when I comprehended, the–horror, I-I shouted something. I don't know what. I knew the shot was meant for me. I sat there, frightened out of my wits. Frightened–"

"You need not be ashamed," offered Hawkes. "It is consistent with the nature of a man not used to violence. Some of what passes for bravery is learned experience. Murder is a monstrous event and one is very rightly horrified by it, even to the point of inaction."

"Thank you," responded Dunmore weakly but with true appreciation. "I-I was–ashamed."

"You shouldn't be. Now, at the time immediately following the tragedy, do you recall what everyone else was doing?"

"I-I can only remember fragments. It is–the blood–that dominates my memory."

"Please try to recall."

"Mrs. Willis was shouting. Yes, she was standing, her hands at the side of her face, screaming. Her husband grabbed her and hugged her to him."

"They were in the room then when the shooting occurred. Who else was in the room with you?"

"Let me see, dinner had ended and some had left the table. Mrs. Hammond, the Willis couple and myself were having a pleasant chat. Over tea. Everyone else was out of the room at the time."

"But with the sound of the shot, they returned. Can you remember at all in what order they returned?"

"No. No I'm sorry. I can't say." Dunmore started to rise but immediately fell back into the cushion of his chair. "My head is whirling. Please, Mr. Hawkes, would you be so kind as to hand me my medicine?" He pointed to a small amber bottle containing a liquid that was sitting on top of a chest of drawers. Simon retrieved it as well as a teaspoon lying beside it and handed both to him.

"Would you like some water?" asked Hawkes as Dunmore opened the bottle and poured a portion of the medicine onto the spoon.

"No, it's not necessary," replied Dunmore, putting the spoon into his mouth and swallowing.

"A few more questions and I'll be off. I've been told it was about an hour before the police arrived. Is that correct?"

"An hour? Yes, I suppose so. It seemed–an eternity."

"You were questioned by the police?"

"Yes. A detective. Named Riley, I believe. "

"And told them, ah, Riley, of the attacks made against you?"

"Certainly."

"Your suspicions of your brother, did you tell the detective of that?"

"N-No, I couldn't implicate him. I-I really don't believe any longer that he's capable of this. He couldn't be."

"Did this Detective Riley state at all his opinion of the crime to you?"

"Only the obvious. What we already know. That poor Mrs. Hammond was accidentally killed by someone making an attempt against my life. Someone who followed me here from New York. He entered the garden by hopping over the back gate and left the same way. More than that, they can't say. Who it is, they haven't a clue."

"No, I suspect not." The limitations of the police and their inability to sort out facts that were less than obvious seemed to be a universal attribute. "Mr. Dunmore, I suggest you leave this house as soon as possible. Your life continues to be in danger and there is no safety here. Perhaps even less refuge than in your own home. I suggest further that you reconsider my suggestion that you hire a bodyguard for your own protection."

"What? Yes, I will leave. And I've already decided to take your suggestion. I've been in contact with an agency in New York. Through them I've hired a bodyguard. He's due here sometime tomorrow. I won't leave until he's come here–to escort me back to the city. I won't go outside my room until then."

"That strikes me as wise," said Hawkes, standing. "I'll leave you now to your rest." As Hawkes was closing the door to the room, Dunmore called out to him, issuing a final plaintive plea: "Mr. Hawkes, please find this man. Please stop him. Please." The words were as much a hoarse cry of pain as they were an appeal and were ladened heavily with the man's internal torment and fear.

CHAPTER FOURTEEN

Hawkes, once more riding the rails of the Ulster &
Delaware Railroad, returning to the metropolis of New York,
dug out a small supply of his shag tobacco, filled his pipe and,
producing a match, lit it up, releasing a cloud of white smoke
into the atmosphere about his face. Alone in the railroad
carriage, there was no one to either object or grant permission to
him for smoking. Immediately he was so engrossed in thought,
silently considering the data that had come his way, that he paid
no attention whatsoever to the splendid scenery streaming past
the window of his carriage. His drawn brows, pulled in tight over
his keen eyes, was proof of his endeavouring to frame all the
possible scenarios which would explain the facts as he now held
them.

Astounding how commonplace was the ability of the police
to misread the facts.

No stranger approached the house from the rear as they had
concluded. No one had bounded over the closed garden gate to
leave the garden grounds after taking his killing shot. No, the
ground spoke against that fiction. The gate was rusted shut and
had not been opened. The police were at least diligent enough to
see that, but then they immediately erred in their assumption that
the killer simply hopped over it. That too could not have
occurred. The ground by the gate spoke against it. If someone
had hopped over the gate there would have been deep
indentations left in the soft earth by his boots as he landed. So
deep that even the footprints of the careless police would not
have erased them. No, it was eminently clear that the gunman
had left another way. Had he climbed over a section of the brick
wall? No, why climb the wall when the shorter gate was
available? Thus, there had to be another way out. That reasoning
had led him to search for another approach in and out of the
garden with the result of his locating the door hidden from sight

behind the thick hedge. The links in his small chain of logic had proven faultless.

A substantive discovery, that door. With it the entire nature of the crime was transformed to the realm of the extraordinary.

He sat almost motionless, his eyes staring vacantly at a spot of the empty seat in front of him, the white smoke from his pipe curling about his stern features. "An ugly business," he murmured softly. "An ugly, ugly business."

It still wanted 10 minutes to the six o'clock hour when Simon found himself again amidst the clamor of sounds which permeated the streets of New York, so much in contrast with the countryside he'd left behind. Here again was the clatter of traffic, the noise of commerce, the hustle of the street venders and the shopkeepers, the hurried movement of the pedestrians and carriages. It was warmer here too, and more humid, again in contrast to the cooler temperatures he'd just left behind.

Small boys, street urchins perhaps nine or ten years of age, positioned themselves in strategic parts of the street outside the train terminal, offering to hail a carriage or sweep paths between the horse droppings in hopes of securing a coin from a gentleman or lady who wanted to avoid soiling their boots or the hem of a long dress. Simon allowed one boy to hail a cab for him and was pleased with the gawking look of amazement that appeared on the boy's grime-streaked face when he pressed a silver dollar into his hand. It was the first time Hawkes had smiled that day.

He dropped his portmanteau off and freshened up at the Dead Rabbits, going to the basin and ewer and splashing some water on his face, washing away the dust of travel. Then, looking at his watch and noting the time, a quarter after the hour now, he left the club and hailed a passing cab on Lafayette. Giving the driver the address of Doctor Rogers' residence and climbing inside the carriage, he settled into the shadow of its interior. In a moment he was on his way and there was only the sharp sound of the horses hooves against the street and the hiss-like churning of the carriage wheels to accompany his thoughts. There were still unknowns in this case, Robert Costes and the good Doctor Rogers among them. Braxton too. He'd request the detectives at the Elizabeth Street precinct to discover what information they could about them, the others as well, paying particular attention to what their past relationships were with Dunmore and the Hammonds.

The air was redolent with the odor of the East River as well as the ever present scent of the horse manure which pockmarked the streets of New York. A cool breeze came through the carriage window and lightly touched Hawkes' cheek. By the half-hour, he was at the well-to-do house where Dr. Rogers retained his practice. The house was preceded by a small yard bounded by a wrought iron fence with a gate that was now open. Hawkes went to the door and, as it too was unlocked–the doctor still accepting patients–went straight inside.

There were subtle signs of opulence inside, the practice apparently flourishing. Seated in the antechamber, waiting to see the doctor, sat a woman and a small child, a girl of about six or seven years of age. The child's face was tinged with red and the eyes were tired. Sick with fever, assessed Simon, looking down at her. They were the only other people in the room.

They were dressed poorly, almost shabbily, and Simon was struck by the incongruity of their appearance and the well-to-do atmosphere of the office. Silently, he questioned how the woman could afford to pay for the doctor's services. The little girl smiled up at Simon, her brown eyes sparkling with mischief despite her illness. She was a pretty little thing. Hawkes returned the smile and the girl turned her face into her mother's bosom to hide.

In the next moment Doctor Rogers entered the room. He was an impressive man of about fifty, a little less than six feet in height, dressed in a finely tailored black suit. His square-jawed countenance evidenced a sense of strong respectability. A man of honour. His cheeks and jowls were covered with grizzled mutton-chop whiskers, a little lighter in colour than his dark brown hair.

Doctor Rogers pulled up abruptly when he saw Hawkes. "Hullo?" he said, scrutinizing him. "Can I help you?" He did not extend his hand.

Hawkes introduced himself and explained the purpose of his visit.

"Ah, yes– shocking–" responded the doctor. "Yes, I'll talk to you but please wait a few minutes, won't you?" He then turned his attention to the woman and the child as Simon took a seat. "How is she?" he asked the mother, his gaze upon the little girl.

"Better, sir," replied the woman, her speech marred by a thick foreign accent.

Doctor Rogers turned to look at the mother. "Come inside. We'll have a look."

Ten minutes passed before the physician, mother and child emerged once again. As the mother and the small girl departed, the doctor again offered his attention to Simon. "Mr., ah, Hawkes, is it?" This time he offered his hand to the detective. "Come inside. We can talk more comfortably there."

The adjoining chamber was a small examination room. Against one wall stood a bookcase containing some medical volumes. A cherry-wood desk was pushed close to the wall opposite the bookcase and the doctor went to the chair behind the desk, at the same time making a motion towards the chair in front of it, indicating that Hawkes should sit there. "I happened to see that little girl on the street with her mother yesterday as I was making my rounds," he told Hawkes as both men sat down. "The child looked sick so I stopped the mother right there and took a quick look at her daughter. She had a fever. I told the mother to get her child home and to bed and then see me today. I told her there'd be no charge to make certain she'd appear. There is so much damned disease in those tenements–something must be done–but happily the girl is looking better today."

"Do you normally stop people on the street like that? inquired Hawkes, impressed by the man's compassion.

"Now and then. When I spot someone who looks ill. They're poor people and would not normally think of taking themselves or their children to a physician. Some of the poor souls survive on an income of–what? two or three hundred dollars a year? But you're not here to hear me prattle on. You're here about poor Amelia's death. What can I do to help you?"

"I would simply appreciate hearing an account of what occurred that night at Black Oak. Exactly as you remember it. If I have any questions I hope you won't mind if I interrupt you with them as they occur to me."

"Not at all."

"But first, may I ask how long you've known George and Amelia Hammond?"

"I've known Amelia since she was a child. I was her parents physician you see. George I know since the marriage to Amelia. Both very healthy. Seldom had any reason to see either one of them at all."

"Were you close with either of them?"

"You mean socially? No, not really."

"How did you come to be invited to Black Oak?"

"That was a bit of a surprise. George had made an appointment for an examination a few days before he was to leave for upstate. During the course of the examination he started talking about his upcoming trip and ended by inviting me to go with him. It was on the spur of the moment."

"I see, now please, if you will, tell me what you remember of that night at Black Oak."

Doctor Rogers offered a crisp succinct account of the events at Black Oak, completing it in brief minutes. The interview yielded nothing new–the doctor's account of the events occurring at Black Oak being in absolute agreement with the others–excepting the unusual bit of news that Dr. Rogers was, in his youth, at the start of his practice, the physician for a time to Franklin Dunmore Senior and Martha Dunmore, the parents of Franklin and Charles Dunmore.

"Just one other thing," said Hawkes as he stood to leave. "Do you own a pistol? For protection on your rounds. I imagine the streets can be pretty rough in some places."

"No, I wouldn't know how to shoot one. I've never had a problem."

Hawkes thanked Rogers for his time and then left the office. A look at his watch gave him the time: still well before seven. He walked to the avenue where his eyes scanned the street for a cab. Not immediately seeing one, he started to walk uptown. The Willis house was not far and he decided the walk would do no harm to his legs.

CHAPTER FIFTEEN

"**M**r. Hawkes?"

Simon responded with a cordial smile. "Yes, it's very kind of you to see me, Mrs. Willis."

Agatha Willis held Hawkes' card in her hand, having just received it from her servant. She glanced at it once more and then lifted her sharp eyes to scrutinize again the man standing before her in her home. "You're a–detective? A private detective?"

"That's correct. I realize the hour is late but I would appreciate a few moments of your time, and your husband's as well, to discuss the incident at Black Oak."

"Benjamin, my husband, isn't here at the moment. He's still at his office."

"Ah, well, may I impose upon only you just now? I can speak to him later if necessary."

Agatha Willis was young, no older than twenty-six, judged Hawkes, and pretty, with striking blue eyes and features which seemed to admirably combine both strength of character and delicacy of form. Her brown hair was pulled back off her forehead and pinned at the back, revealing an intelligent high brow. Her mouth was firm but saved from severity by a suggestion of compassion, of sensitivity.

"That will be all, James," she said, dismissing the manservant who had shown Hawkes in. "Please sit down, Mr. Hawkes. Certainly I'll help you any way I can." She placed herself in a plush Queen Anne near a window and indicated the chair opposite her for Hawkes. He went over and sat in it.

"I thought all detectives were employed either by the Police Department or by Pinkerton," she said to him.

"Not all, Mrs. Willis. I work alone."

Sadness appeared in Mrs. Willis' remarkable eyes. "I will miss Amelia. She was almost–like an older sister to me. I only knew her little more than a year, but in that time we had become close friends. Her strong interest, as you may know, is, was, the fight for women's rights–suffrage–and she inspired in me the desire to fight for that too. We have formed a small group which we hope will be influential in that fight. She will be missed. She was a driving force." Agatha produced a handkerchief and wiped two incipient tears from the corners of her eyes. "She cared so much for others. She would actually cry sometimes when she spoke of the working conditions of women here in the factories– the garment industry–the women who sew our clothes–slavery– nothing less–right here in New York, years after the Civil War. Years after the slaves were freed. The poor people, helpless and exploited by those in positions of power. The women work for seventy hours a week, for no more than twenty or thirty cents a day. Amelia was determined to change things for the better. Now she's gone."

"It is a worthy cause," said Hawkes. "Man's ability to exploit others for gain is well known to me. If there's any hope for change, it resides, as always, in the hearts of compassionate and courageous people. There will be no better testament to Mrs. Hammond than a victory for your group."

"Thank you, Mr. Hawkes. We will go on trying–despite the threats."

"Threats?"

"Most certainly. The owners refuse to recognize any rights for their workers and reject any suggestion that they should. There was more than one factory owner angry with her. With us. But the rights of Labour must be recognized. She was trying to get the women to unionize, to fight back against their mistreatment. And she was trying to get laws passed, to have the government legislate a minimum wage for the workers." Mrs. Willis shook her head rather sadly. "Last year's defeat in Pennsylvania was disheartening for those of us interested in workers' rights. The governor there had no business sending in the state militia to protect the strike breakers. Amelia was very upset over that for his actions there set back the cause here as well. The Pinkertons too were on the wrong side there. I think if you were from Pinkerton I would have sent you away."

"It is my good fortune then that I am not," returned Hawkes with a smile. "Please, I would like to hear your statement of what happened at Black Oak. I ask you to be as precise as you can be in your telling of it. It may prove to be helpful in capturing her killer."

"I will do my best."

Agatha Willis was only a few sentences into her narrative when there came into the room the sound of a heavy step in the hall. Both Hawkes and Mrs. Willis turned towards the sound just as Benjamin Willis appeared in the doorway. His face bore a harried expression that vanished and was replaced by a friendly smile when he saw Hawkes. "Hullo?" He turned to his wife. "You have a guest?"

"This is Mr. Simon Hawkes, a detective. He's come about–poor Amelia."

"Oh, I see." He stepped forward and extended his hand. "Terrible business, that."

Benjamin Willis was almost six feet tall and athletically built. His youthful, pleasant face was topped with a head of thick, brown hair. He was dressed to the point of impressiveness and his large heavy-lidded eyes smiled at Hawkes as the two shook hands. "This is a bit of good luck," said Simon. "I was prepared to return later to meet you but now that you're here, you can save me that trip. If you can afford me a few minutes?"

"A few minutes? Certainly, but that's all I'll be able to give you. I am in a rush. I only came home to get some papers I have here. I need them at my office."

"I understand you to be an attorney. Is that how you came to be acquainted with George Hammond–through your profession?"

"Yes, but acquaintances is all we are. We're not friends at all. It's my wife and Amelia who were close." His gaze turned sympathetic as he glanced over to his wife. "It was quite a shock–to lose a good friend and to witness–something like that as well. My wife was shaking like a leaf hours afterward." His gaze then floated to the clock on the mantle. "Mr. Hawkes, I really do have only a few minutes."

"Yes, of course. It won't take long. Your wife has just begun to relate to me the events of that night. You need only stay and listen. Please feel free to interrupt at any point if you feel it's necessary. Otherwise I will take your silence as your agreement to her statement. Now, please, Mrs. Willis, begin again."

With a nod of her head, Agatha began once more to relate the events of that terrible night. At one point in the telling, she burst into tears and had to be comforted by her husband, who went and sat on the arm of the Queen Anne by her side. In her speaking of the moment when Amelia Hammond had been fatally shot, the full horror of it returned vividly before her and she could not help but shed tears at the memory of it. It was a few moments before she could go on.

"I-I'm sorry," she murmured to Hawkes as she composed herself.

"There's no need to apologize," commented her husband. Then, turning to Hawkes, "It was horrendous. I remember watching it as it happened—in disbelief. It couldn't be happening, I thought. Then my stomach turned over when I realized it was indeed happening. Terrible. I understand the shot was intended for that Dunmore fellow. He was absolutely terrified afterwards. Can't say I blame him. How's he faring?"

"As well as possible—given the circumstances."

"And Hammond. How is he?"

"I'm told he's taken it rather badly. He's under a doctor's care. Doctor Rogers."

"Poor fellow—the way he carried on—"

Fresh tears fell from Agatha Willis eyes and she dabbed them away. "I'm sorry," she apologized once more.

"Are you certain you can go on?" asked her husband.

With a deep intake of breath and a stiffening of her back, Agatha declared her intention of doing so. She continued uninterrupted until finished.

"Did either of you see anything unusual while at Black Oak? Anything at all? A stranger by the house for example?"

Both husband and wife shook their heads. "No, nothing, Mr. Hawkes," voiced Benjamin Willis, speaking for both of them. Then, standing, he said, "Pardon me, but now I really must be off. I must get back to my office. It was a pleasure to meet you, sir." He turned to his wife. "My papers–they'll be upstairs?"

Agatha nodded her head and he turned again to Hawkes. "Good-bye. I wish you the best of luck in tracking down this killer." He turned on his heels immediately so that when Hawkes said good-bye in return he was speaking to the man's departing back, Willis being already half-way out of the room.

"And thank you, Mrs. Willis," said Hawkes as he raised himself out of his chair, "for accepting this late intrusion. I wonder, may I make one additional imposition? Would you have a list of names of those factory owners your group has petitioned on behalf of their workers? Could you indicate those among them who issued threats as well?"

"W-Why, yes, of course. You don't think–"

"You did mention that Mrs. Hammond had received threats. I would be remiss if I did not learn who it was who issued those threats."

"It will take a little time to get all the names together."

"Please, have someone deliver it to The Dead Rabbits Society. I'm staying there. You know of it?"

"Yes, a men's only club on Lafayette."

"Thank you. And again I wish you success in your group's cause. It is a noble one. If I can be of any assistance, please contact me. I will be happy to help."

"Thank you." She smiled appreciatively. "That's very kind."

"I'll show myself out. Good night."

Outside, dusk was creeping to night, the sky above began rumbling with the threat of rain and Simon saw clouds the colour of grey stone beginning to press down upon the rooftops. Rain appeared suddenly eminent but there was one more interview to achieve this night and Hawkes saw no reason to let the threat of

97

rain keep him from it. He hailed a carriage over to him and, climbing inside, gave the driver the address of the apartment of Robert Costes.

In attempting to meet with Robert Costes that evening, Hawkes would be disappointed. The young man was not at home when he called. The interview of the young man would now unfortunately have to be delayed a time as Hawkes would not be able to devote further effort to Dunmore's problem. For the next few days at least, his obligation to the city's Police Commissioner, a man in danger of having his reputation forever polluted and his career ruined by a Milverton-like blackmailer, had to be fulfilled. The success of that case now demanded his full time and attention.

As Hawkes rode in the carriage, returning to the Dead Rabbits, his thoughts yielded up to him the last image he held of the terrified Franklin Dunmore. He saw again the man's fearful face as he issued his pitiable plea that he, Hawkes, identify and halt the threat against him. That threat, if Hawkes was correct, and he held no doubt that he was, was more real now than previously. It was well and good that the frightened man had decided to obtain a bodyguard for the sake of securing his safety. Another attempt would most certainly be made against his life, this time with a more serious and purposeful effort to put a final end to it.

CHAPTER SIXTEEN

At ten past eight that night, as Hawkes was on his way to the Elizabeth Street police precinct, Robert Costes was walking towards the East Side of the city, towards the tenements and the poverty into which he'd been born. Glancing up at the sky he saw that its clear visage was slowly being conquered by dark clouds threatening rain, stretching like the talons of some large creature, as though wanting to grasp and hold the setting sun. He understood the frustration of those clouds, did Robert Costes, the frustration of wanting things which were unattainable, or least appeared so.

He experienced a sense of distaste as he trod through the shabby, grimy streets of the neighbourhood in which his parents still lived. Soon, with hard work and luck, he would be able to afford to get them out, away from here, to a better place.

His parents were both Italian immigrants who had entered the country as man and wife thirty years earlier. The name he'd given himself, Robert Costes, was a twist of his own true name, Roberto Costispoti. He was not ashamed of his heritage–proud of it, in fact–but he was mortified of the poverty from which he came and was astute enough an observer of the human condition to know there existed in the world prejudice against his race, prejudice which would hinder him in his making a living. It was easier to avoid it than confront it.

It was a month since his last visit and he was surprised, unhappily, when he saw his mother. She seemed a little older, thinner, shrunken. Was her hair more streaked with grey than last time?

She greeted him warmly, cradling his face in her rough hands as though he was still a little boy and gazing at him with tears in her pleased eyes. "Roberto," she murmured, standing on her toes as he bent down to her so that she could kiss him on the forehead. He was, as always, touched by the strength of the love she held for him. Of her three sons and one daughter, he was her firstborn and her favourite. All of her sons were still alive. Her daughter was deceased, a suicide, leaping off the Brooklyn Bridge in a moment of profound despair.

His father was a bull, sixty-four years of age, still strong and powerful although thicker about the waist than even a few years previous, with a dark complexioned broad face. His black hair, without a touch of grey, was greased and parted in the middle. He had fine prominent brown eyes and a slightly aquiline nose. A meat dealer with a small shop on Hester Street, he toiled, and still laboured most days, twelve or more hours each day. One of his achievements, the one of which he was most proud, was his having succeeded in paying for a quality education for his eldest son, Roberto, "the small one with the brains". His other two sons showed no interest in "living in books" which was fortunate, for there was no way the family finances could stand the strain of granting them the education given the first-born boy. The shop didn't bring in enough money for that.

His father's voice came out to him from the kitchen. "Come in. Sit." When Roberto entered, his father gave him a broad smile of welcome.

Roberto–Robert Costes–was aware of the sacrifices his father had made for him. Money was scarce. Still he experienced a sense of distaste at the common appearance, the lack of graceful manners, of his parents. He almost always experienced a kind of shrinking of his heart, a slight hostility, when he came here to this dingy series of grim rooms into which he'd been born. He wasn't sure why he felt this way. Perhaps it was shame–or vanity.

Still he loved his parents, his family. Loved them despite being unable to summon the ability to be proud of them. How could he be proud of them? He would make the best of it, and endure what they were.

"Hullo, Papa," he said, smiling in response to his father's smile. "How are you?"

"Better than all the Caesars. They're dead. Come. Sit. Talk."

Robert installed himself in the chair opposite his father. "Where're Fabio, and Nick?" he asked.

"Still at the shop. They'll be home soon."

"I can only stay a little while," said Robert.

His father grunted. "You look good. So tell me what you been doing," he demanded in a friendly hearty tone. "You want something to eat?"

"No, nothing." Robert inhaled deeply, deciding to get straight to the point of his visit. "Papa, this Friday–is Angela's birthday. On Sunday, I want to go to her grave. I want you to come with me. With me and Mama.'"

His father's face darkened. "I told you–"

"She was your daughter, Papa," protested Robert, insisting.

The elder Costispoti glared at him. "I have no daughter."

"Papa, you can't keep saying that," declared Robert, his voice rising, the tone containing some contempt for his father's stubbornness. "She was my sister, and she was your daughter. She's dead, Papa. If she made a mistake, it's time to forgive her for it."

"Never!" His father's voice caught fire. "Her soul is burning in hell for what she did! Never!"

The two men, father and son, began to argue and, in the adjoining room, listening to their angry words, sat Robert's mother, now sobbing silent and suffering tears.

CHAPTER SEVENTEEN

It was on the afternoon of the third day following Hawkes first attempt to interview Robert Costes, that he at last achieved a satisfactory conclusion to the troubling affair revolving about the commissioner of police, rescuing that man's reputation from irreparable damage. Falling back upon his amazing ability to dissemble and alter his appearance (Hawkes' skills were such that they would have enabled him to achieve a fine career as a stage actor) and utilizing the same stratagem as he had in London against Irene Adler years previous, this time with more success than against that respected adversary, he was able to retrieve the damaging document, thus rendering the blackmailer toothless and subject to immediate arrest.

Hawkes had little time to enjoy that small victory as that very evening he once again found himself in a landau making his way to the home of Robert Costes. His thoughts, during the past three days, had at times turned to Franklin Dunmore and the unusual danger which swirled about the frightened man. He was aware that no harm had as yet befallen Dunmore as he'd requested detectives at the Elizabeth Street Police Precinct to check upon the man each day and report to him immediately if an attack had occurred. Not hearing from the police he was satisfied that all was well for the time being.

To his disappointment, the police failed as of yet to supply him with any new information regarding Hammond's servants and the guests present at Black Oak at the time of Amelia Hammond's murder. He wanted to learn more about each of their histories for he was certain that it would be there, in one of those personal archives, that he would find the true direction leading to the solution of the mystery.

Robert Costes resided in a brick apartment building leasing its rooms to people of moderate means. One of a line of buildings on what had once been a fashionable street but which had over the past decade descended somewhat in stature. While well above the quality of the building in which his parents lived, the residence was leagues beneath the true luxury Costes desired. For now though, it was the best he could afford. Indeed, the rental here was a bit more than that, as his obtaining his lodgings even here placed a strain upon his salary.

This time, rapping upon Costes' dun-coloured apartment door, Hawkes was greeted with the sound of the young man's voice responding to his knock.

In the next instant, the door was opened and there was Costes, clad in trousers and shirt, his jacket and tie discarded for the evening. After introducing himself, Hawkes was invited to come inside.

Costes' apartment was composed of three good-sized rooms which were tastefully if somewhat sparsely furnished. A bookcase stood against one wall between two windows, its shelves dotted with volumes. The young man enjoys his reading, concluded Hawkes, and is in the process of building his library. A roll-top desk sat in one corner and, on the desk, resided a Remington typewriter. An expensive mechanical device.

Hawkes' keen eyes took in the young man. Costes' face was composed of pleasant enough features, and contained an intellectual quality that was emphasized by the small, oval-shaped gold-framed eyeglasses he wore. The brown eyes behind the lenses were bright and alert.

A small meal, a piece of trout, half-eaten, and some vegetables were on a plate on the dining table. A glass of white wine, half-empty, stood near the dish. If Robert Costes was inclined to resent Hawkes interruption of his meal, he gave no evidence of it, greeting him with cordiality and a smile.

"Please accept my apologies for interrupting your supper," said Simon as he placed himself in the chair offered by Costes.

The young man waved the apology away. "I was finished anyway. The piece of fish is a little too large for me. I don't believe in eating too heavy a meal. Now, you said you were here about poor Mrs. Hammond. What can I do to help you?"

"If you will, please tell me, being as precise as you can, exactly what happened at Black Oak the night Mrs. Hammond was killed."

"Have you spoken to the others who were there?"

Hawkes replied that he had.

"Well, then you must already know that I was out of the room when Mrs. Hammond was killed. Thank God I wasn't there. Ghastly. I left right after dinner. They were serving cakes, coffee and tea, but I had already eaten too much. I excused myself and went up to my room. There isn't much, other than that, that I can say, I think."

"You went directly to your room?"

"Well, no, I did stop briefly in the library. There's an excellent library there and I'm an avid reader. I got a copy of "Daisy Miller", by Henry James and went up to read it. I had barely gotten to my room when I heard the shot. I didn't know what it was at first."

"What did you do when you heard it?"

"Well, nothing at first. I wasn't sure at all where it came from–or even that it was a gunshot. It wasn't until I heard the screams that I realized something–something terrible–had taken place. After some hesitation, I went back down to the dining room–and saw Mrs. Hammond. I very nearly passed out at the sight. There was blood–all over the table. It was clear that there was nothing to be done to save her. Poor Mr. Hammond was quite distraught. The doctor and Huxley had all they could do to pull him away from her. Then Braxton came through the French Doors. He startled me–frightened me to be honest about it–waving his pistol about. I thought at first it was Mrs. Hammond's killer coming into the room to shoot us all. I literally jumped back at the sight of him."

"And then?"

"Well, there's not much to say. They, Huxley and Doctor Rogers, asked everyone to leave the room and the two of them covered Mrs. Hammond's head, with one or two of the large napkins. They couldn't just leave her there like that. Mr.

Hammond was taken to his room–put to bed. We all went into the parlor and waited there while Braxton went for the police."

"Did you see anything during your stay at Black Oak, anything at all, which might be of significance. Anything, no matter how trivial?"

Costes reflected for a moment and shook his head. "No, there's nothing comes to mind. Sorry."

"You saw no strangers for example. No one on or near the property who didn't belong?"

"Absolutely no one. I stayed in the garden, reading, most of the time. It was very pleasant there. I didn't go about much."

"How long have you worked for Mr. Hammond?"

"Not long. Just a few weeks actually."

"Um, he's only known you a short time and yet he extended an invitation to his country home to you?"

"Yes, I was surprised when he invited me. But I was working on a case in which he had a strong interest. He told me that my coming along would allow him to mix a bit of business with pleasure. I'd like to think also that Mr. Hammond was showing an interest in me due to the quality of my work. He expressed an appreciation for my work when he recruited me from the law firm of Drury and Cummings. That's where I was employed when he hired me."

"He recruited you?"

Costes sat a bit straighter, a bit taller in his chair, permitting himself some pride. "Yes, he came to me saying he'd heard good things about my work. That his firm was always looking out for employees with talent and that he'd like to have me with his firm. Offered me a good increase in salary so of course I accepted right off."

"I couldn't help but notice the Remington typewriter on your desk there. I suppose your salary increase enabled you to purchase it?"

"That? No, it's too expensive. They cost over a hundred dollars. That doesn't belong to me. It's supplied to me by the firm. You see, I often work at home and the firm has recently instituted a policy that all papers must be typewritten. Problems deciphering some of the poorer scripts, you see. I didn't like it at first but now I rather enjoy it. Once you get the hang of it, it's quite simple."

"Is it?"

"That's the latest model. It actually has a shift-key to let you type in lower case, and it's a visible writer. You can see what you're typing without having to lift the carriage. Ingenious really."

"Yes, it seems we live in an age of wonders. Everyday something new comes along to astound us. Well, I won't take any more of your time," added Hawkes, pushing himself out of the chair. "Do you know the location of The Dead Rabbits Society?"

"Yes, I do. I was invited there once for lunch by Mr. Hammond."

"Good, if you think of anything else which may be of assistance to me, please don't hesitate to contact me there. Good-night."

"Mr. Hawkes, may I ask, how is Mr. Hammond? I understand he's absolutely devastated by what happened, to the point where it's affecting his health. We are all, at the firm, concerned for him."

"To my knowledge he continues to recover under his doctor's care," replied Hawkes. "I will, when next I see him, relay your concern to him. Good-night."

Outside the building, Hawkes was frowning thoughtfully, digesting the information Costes had given him, searching for but failing to see the gleam of light he was seeking to break through the haze of shadows surrounding the case. He grunted with disappointment and then, on the moment, decided to call upon Franklin Dunmore. Dunmore's home wasn't a great distance from the Costes apartment and the night had brought with it an exhilarating nip to the air. Hawkes decided to eschew the use of the waiting carriage, paid the driver, and started walking towards Broadway.

As he went up the steps to the entrance of Dunmore's home, he saw that the door was unlocked and left slightly ajar. Immediately a coldness brushed against his spine and he withdrew his revolver. Applying some slight pressure to the door he nudged it open, slowly, cautiously. "Dunmore?" he called out. There was no answer but simply the continuance of the unnatural silence. Hawkes entered the house, then stepped through the small foyer and pressed himself against the wall of the corridor into which it led.

Here he stood and listened intently, hearing nothing excepting the melancholy tick of the pendulum of the mantle clock in the nearby room. He was about to step forward when he was halted by a sudden flicker of movement at the opposite end of the hall which grabbed his attention. A shifting movement in the dark shadows. Hawkes faced it in a slight crouch, his pistol aimed towards the darkness, ready to fire.

A man, squat and stocky in build, emerged from the dark, walking slowly into the light. The eyes of the man were opened wide in shock and desperation. His mouth moved as though he was attempting to speak but hadn't the strength for words. He was severely wounded, the front of his white shirt was soaked red and blood covered his chest like a scarlet cravat. He halted, leaned heavily against the wall of the passageway and, in an effort to balance himself, pressed a hand upon a small table which stood nearby. It lacked the strength to hold his bulk and, the thin legs snapping like twigs, both table and man went crashing to the floor.

Hawkes, still cautious, went to him. The man's eyes were shining and wide open, but unseeing and vacant. Putting two fingertips to the man's neck, Hawkes sought to feel a pulse but found none.

Dunmore's hired bodyguard? No doubt. His pistol, a Colt, was still holstered. He'd been caught unawares. Assassins do not enter houses without their weapons drawn. The hush in the house was palpable, as though the very atmosphere was holding its breath, startled by the presence of death.

Hawkes made a hurried but careful search of the floor, concerned that an intruder might still be present. Then, satisfied there was no one in concealment in any of the rooms on the first floor, he ascended the stairs to the second. Here he discovered the body of Franklin Dunmore sprawled on the floor of his bedroom, his legs splayed, a bullet in the back of his head. Blood and bits of bone were splashed and scattered on the floor. Dunmore's face was a mask of fear and horror, the eyes wide and staring, questioning, as though unable to comprehend the truth of the death which had come to him. His hand was stretched out as that of a man beseeching assistance, but assistance was well beyond being of service to Dunmore now.

The smell of gunpowder was absent. The murder had occurred some time ago. Still, Hawkes made a quick search of the rest of the house and then, finding it empty as he expected, returned to Dunmore's bedroom. There to make an efficient examination of it and the hall and stairs leading to it. He discovered nothing of significance, achieving only a continuation of his own frustration. Following his inspection of the premises, he left the house to summon the police to the grim scene.

Discontentment held Hawkes in its tight grip as he returned to his room at the Dead Rabbits later that night. He was deeply dissatisfied with himself, with his inability, which he viewed as a personal failing, to save Dunmore from death.

Then, arising out from the midst of that discontent, for no reason that Hawkes could name, he saw again the grounds of the garden of the house known as Black Oak. The gaze of his mind's eye focused, with a kind of ferocity, upon the one new object he'd seen in the garden many days ago, the gleaming sundial that sat in its centre, sparkling in the sunlight.

He decided on the moment, to return to Black Oak, obtaining passage on the first available train in the morning.

CHAPTER EIGHTEEN

"Fool!"

Hawkes, having discovered what he'd expected to find at Black Oak, now, and for the entire journey of his return to New York City, berated himself for his lack of insight during his initial trip to Hammond's country home. The case was a simple one and his own shortcomings had failed to spot the obvious. He'd failed Dunmore also. If he'd had his wits about him at that time, the man might still be alive. The internal sting of guilt prodded him to further murmured insults against himself. What would Watson do with this tale of incompetence? "How blind I have been! Imbecile! I deserve to be kicked all the way from New York to the American frontier. Idiot!"

It was mid-afternoon when Hawkes returned to the Dead Rabbits. To his surprise, a detective he was friendly with, Detective Cullen working out of the Elizabeth Street Precinct, arrived only minutes after he did, seeking him out. A knock on the door of his room brought him and Cullen face to face.

"Mr. Hawkes," said the detective, a broad smile on his face. "You asked me to keep you informed of any happenings in the Dunmore case. Well, it's done. Solved. We have a confession."

"Confession?" responded Hawkes, surprised.

"A death-bed confession of sorts," responded Cullen. He was a flaxen-haired man with a pugnacious nose that sat above a blond-red moustache like a street-tough drinking pints at a table in a pub and he was evidently very pleased to be able to close the book on this little investigation. The edges of his moustache seemed to want to turn up in an attempt to smile as well. "A man named Robert Costes. He's been found hanged, a suicide in his room. He's left behind a complete confession regarding his murdering the Dunmore fellow. Case closed."

Although the occurrences have been seldom, I have witnessed astonishment on the face of Sherlock Holmes on more than one instance. I have detailed the most notable of these occasions in the reminiscences entitled "A Scandal in Bohemia" and "The Hound of the Baskervilles". In each instance, it occurred when the criminal he pursued behaved in a manner he had not foreseen. I have no doubt that his reaction now, upon hearing the words of Detective Cullen, was similar, although, when relating the event to me years later, he simply told me, after releasing a cloud of smoke from his cherrywood pipe, in his rather matter-of-fact manner, that the death of Robert Costes was "quite unexpected".

Costes had failed to appear at his desk for work that morning. An absence that caused some inconvenience to his office as he was scheduled to bring in some important legal papers he had reviewed at home the previous evening. One of Costes' co-workers, a man of twenty-three years of age named Howard Lethbridge, was selected to go round and rouse him up, to see what was wrong and obtain the needed documents. Lethbridge accepted the task willingly, the sun was shining, the sky was clear and it was a pleasure to be free of the drudgery of the office even if just for a few minutes. Robert Costes' apartment was only minutes walking distance from George Hammond's law office and so Lethbridge was there in no time at all. Even with his stopping at a local bar for a quick beer. Reaching the door, he knocked and waited, and received no response. He knocked again and again and still the same. With the admonition of his superior ringing in his ears ("Don't come back without those papers!") he sought out the superintendent of the building and had him open the apartment door. The sight that greeted the men as they stepped into the apartment horrified them. There, suspended by a length of rope in the centre of the room, his eyes opened and protruding grotesquely as though ready to pop right out of his skull, was the lifeless body of Robert Costes.

His features stamped now with horror, Lethbridge backed out of the room. He left the superintendent and ran off, screaming for the police.

Hawkes and Cullen exited the Dead Rabbits and went to the waiting carriage. Both men climbed into it and, with a shouted command from Cullen, the carriage pulled away and entered into the stream of traffic. Simon's mind was racing, analyzing what little he knew of Costes, trying to determine exactly how the young man fit into the complex events surrounding the death of Franklin Dunmore.

"Are you certain it's suicide?" he inquired.

"Certain as rain," replied Cullen. "He was discovered a little bit after ten this morning. Me and one of my men went up and found him hanging from his chandelier like a goose in a Chinese butcher shop. We found a letter he wrote on one of those new-fangled contraptions they have now, a typewriter. It was his confession as well as his farewell to the world. He confessed to killing both Amelia Hammond and Frank Dunmore. Gave his reasons in the letter. My men have been busy as bees verifying the facts as written and we're satisfied. Costes is our murderer, pure and simple. And he hanged himself, pure and simple as well."

Hawkes sniffed sardonically. The two men rode in silence the rest of the distance to the building in which Costes had lived, with Hawkes' face as grim as Cullen's was pleased.

The apartment was exactly as Simon recalled it, neat and orderly, respectable. Two new objects however now greeted his eyes. There, on the kitchen table was a medical bag, beside it lay a pistol, a Smith & Wesson .44. Cullen noticed Simon's eyes fasten upon the bag and the pistol. "It's you told us the man used a medical bag to get about with the least amount of notice on the part of others. There it is. And there's your Smith & Wesson as well. You were right about that too."

"Small solace," murmured Hawkes. "You're certain he's your man?"

"Yes, though I can't claim any credit for knowing it. Seeing as how he cleared it all up himself. It's all in the note he left behind. Between you, me and the walls, Mr. Hawkes, it's a good thing he decided to bear his soul. I don't think we'd ever have put handcuffs on him. Now of course, with his confession, it's all clear as crystal."

"Is it?"

"No doubt. You want to hear the long of it?"

"Of course."

Cullen waved a hand towards the small table where Costes had enjoyed his dinner of the previous night. Fish and vegetables, a glass of wine. "We'll sit," said Cullen. "For some reason it's easier to talk sitting than standing."

The two men sat at the table and Cullen, pulling over a tumbler to use as an ashtray, lit up a cigar.

"We–the police–were notified at about ten-thirty this morning that this fellow was discovered in his apartment hanging by his neck. It was determined from the rigidity of the muscles that he'd been dead about ten hours give or take. Probably did himself at sometime between eleven last night and two this morning."

"Discovered? Who discovered him?"

"Another clerk in the firm where he worked. It seems this Costes fellow was working on some important papers and had taken them home to finish them up. When he didn't arrive at his desk this morning–he is, I'm told, always very punctual–the others in the office said they could set their watches by him– when he failed to show this morning, they sent someone around to him and there he was."

"How did this other fellow get into the apartment?"

"Got the superintendent to let him in."

Hawkes grunted. "When you arrived you found a note?"

"We did. Good thing too. Otherwise, as I said, we'd not have connected this with the murder of Dunmore. It was a typewritten note, three pages in length, and went into detail explaining why he'd murdered Dunmore and then expressing his sorrow over the accidental killing of Amelia Hammond. He had no remorse over killing Dunmore–the man got what he earned, he wrote–but Mrs. Hammond was an innocent victim and just as justice demanded Dunmore pay for his crime, so should he–Costes–pay for his."

"I confess to being stunned," stated Hawkes. "Dunmore had to pay for his crime? What crime could that man possibly have committed against Costes? Against anyone, for that matter?"

Cullen's engaging smile returned. "Ah, that is the surprise, isn't it? Well, it seems that Dunmore was not the totally quiet soul he appeared to be. It turns out he had an affair a while back– with a young woman he employed in his home as a maid. They carried it on, very discreetly, for a few months, until the girl discovered she was pregnant. She wanted marriage of course but Dunmore wanted none of that and just wanted to be done with her. The woman ended up by killing herself, throwing herself off the Brooklyn Bridge. She's that same girl we had you come take a look at a while back, remember?"

Hawkes replied that he recalled the incident very well.

"It turns out that she was Costes' younger sister. When Costes discovered it was Dunmore who misused her, he blamed him for her death. It turns out that Costes is not even his real name. He was born of parents named Costispoti. Immigrants. They live over on the East Side, on Hester Street."

"You astound me."

"His parents told me that he changed his name for the sake of his career. I was at the parent's flat earlier today. They took the news of his death hard. They had high hopes for him. Sacrificed to give him a quality education. Now their dreams for him are gone. They just sat and cried most of the time I was there. I'm satisfied they had nothing to do with this." Cullen took a puff from his cigar and released the smoke slowly, letting it curl out from his barely parted lips. "We've already verified the facts as far as we're able," he continued. "A young woman by the name of Angela Costispoti was employed by Dunmore. A little less than one year after first beginning work for him, she was discovered floating in the East River. A postmortem examination on her showed she was months pregnant at the time of her death."

"That proves she had an affair with someone. Has anyone linked Angela Costispoti with Dunmore as lovers?"

"So far no one. We're making inquires. But I don't think it's necessary to get that kind of corroboration. The facts are clear and straightforward. Roberto Costispoti's sister had an affair with Dunmore. He refused to marry her. Driven to despair she committed suicide. Somehow Roberto Costispoti found out it was Dunmore who was his dead sister's lover and he held him responsible for her death. He then went after him to avenge her." Cullen ended his statement with a slight shrug of his shoulders.

"It all fits together remarkably well," stated Hawkes.

"Clear as crystal. Even his change of name came in handy now, for Dunmore wouldn't associate Robert Costes with the girl he'd wronged, Angela Costispoti. He went after Dunmore, failed in his first attempts, during one of which he ended by accidentally killing Mrs. Hammond. To his credit, after he at last obtained his revenge and killed Dunmore, he extracted the same punishment from himself, that is, he executed himself as well."

"Clear as crystal, as you say. Still, it's a bit difficult to imagine that prim and proper man, Franklin Dunmore, having an illicit affair. Would you mind if I looked about?"

"Help yourself. Except for the body being removed. everything is pretty much as it was when we got here." Cullen remained seated, watching Hawkes and puffing on his cigar as Simon went about the room. "I'm acquainted with you a short time, Mr. Hawkes, but I know you well enough to know you'd want to do one of your examinations. Although there's not much to find here, I wager."

Hawkes gazed at the chair laying on its side a few feet from being directly beneath the chandelier. Near the chair, also on the floor, was the thick rope that had transported Costes from this world to the next. It had been cut from the mantle so that Costes could be lowered to the floor.

"So he looped the rope over the chandelier, fastened one end to the mantle there, climbed up on the chair, placed the noose around his neck, and stepped off. Is that how you see it?"

"Precisely," replied Cullen.

"Why is the chair such a distance away then?"

114

"I questioned that myself. The way I see it, he stepped off the chair, at the same time kicking it away with a swipe of his foot so that he wouldn't be able to step on it again. In the event he had a change of mind while dangling at the end of the rope."

"Yes, that's possible." Simon picked up the long length of rope and, producing a magnifying lens from his pocket, scrutinized it. "Helloa, what have we here?" he murmured.

Cullen's ears perked up. "What? Do you see something?"

"I see once again that I should have more faith. When a fact opposes a string of deductions, it is invariably the fact that is questionable. When Costes was lowered down, his feet were held. He was not lowered by someone using the rope, that's so, is it not.?"

"Yes, I myself held his legs. One of my men cut the rope over there by the mantle and I lowered him down. How do you know that?"

Hawkes tossed the rope over to the seated detective. "Have a look at that," he said as he stepped over to Costes' desk.

Cullen gazed at the rope and then back at Hawkes in confusion. "Look at it? What for?"

Hawkes ignored the question and Cullen relapsed into concerned silence. The suicide letter lay on the desk and Hawkes picked it up and took some minutes to read it. Then, placing the three pages aside, he began an examination of the desk itself and its other contents.

"Those legal papers you mentioned," he asked, without looking away from the desk. "Do you know if they've been returned to the law firm?"

"W-Why yes, I saw no harm. This fellow–named Griffin–Costes' supervisor there–insisted they were needed. I turned them over."

"Do you know if they were worked on by Costes?"

"As a matter of fact they were finished up by him. This fellow Griffin seemed quite pleased by that. I don't think he minded Costes' death so much once he knew the work was done."

115

Hawkes, completing his examination, returned to the table and sat down. "And what did you make of that?" he asked. Wouldn't it be unusual for a man who is contemplating suicide to consider it a strong necessity that he complete his work for the following day?"

Cullen frowned. "I-I must admit–I didn't consider it."

Hawkes smiled. "Well, in fact, it needn't be indicative of anything at all. Human beings are nothing if not self-contradictory and inconsistent. The detective who prizes logic too highly in regards to human behavior may find himself more puzzled than not at times. Suicides can do very unusual things. I recall one woman who sewed the buttons on her husband's shirts and mended her children's socks just prior to cutting her wrists."

Cullen's own smile returned. "Ah, you were making me nervous there, Mr. Hawkes. I imagined you thought maybe this Costispoti fellow didn't hang himself as is clear he did."

"Oh, well that is obvious. What we have here a clear case of murder, Cullen. Pure and simple."

Cullen's mouth dropped open so that the cigar it held very nearly fell into his lap. "M-Murder! The devil you say–" His face wore the incredulous expression of a child witnessing for the first time the incomprehensible trick of a practiced conjurer. "Th-That can't be!"

"It cannot be anything else. The fact that the note was typewritten rather than given in Costes' own hand is immediately suggestive that it may have been written by someone else, is it not?"

"It isn't proof of anything, is it?" protested Cullen. "Costes himself might have done it. Why not typewrite a suicide note?"

"I did say it was only suggestive. However, there are two pieces of evidence which are irrefutable. Are you aware, Cullen, of the individuality of typewriting machines?"

"Individuality?" responded a befuddled Cullen.

"Yes, unless new, a typewriter may have as much individuality as a person's handwritten script. No two are exactly alike as the letters do not wear the same. If you notice, on

Costes' desk there remain some papers he typed on the Remington there. I've noted a few characteristics of the machine that appear on them, a slight defect in the letter g, the same in the letter u. There are others as well. I have given some thought to writing a monograph on the subject of the typewriter and crime. I continue to procrastinate in the doing of it."

"I don't understand what you're getting at, Mr. Hawkes," complained Cullen.

"Simply this, the suicide letter does not contain these characteristics I've mentioned. Therefore it was not written on that machine."

"What?" Cullen was flabbergasted.

"I said there were two conclusive pieces of evidence that murder has occurred here. The other is the rope you have on your lap. If you examine it closely you will see that the small fibers of that portion of the rope which passed over the bar of the chandelier are bent in the direction going *towards* the noose. That can only mean one thing, that Costes was pulled up on the rope rather than dropping down. If he had committed suicide or was lowered by the rope the fibers would be bent in the opposite direction, away from the noose. It is simplicity itself."

"Murder?"

"A very cold-blooded murder. By a man who is fiendishly clever, and profoundly evil. This last homicide was intended to give the police a finish to their investigation in the killings of Mrs. Hammond and Dunmore and thus rescue the true assassin from any concern that he might in time be discovered. He left his Smith & Wesson and medical bag here to complete the illusion that Robert Costes was the killer. Perhaps using the threat of that very pistol, the Smith & Wesson, he forced Costes to place the noose around his neck. Then he very cold-bloodedly pulled him up off the ground, letting the young man strangle to death. Our killer than kicked over the chair and took out the sham suicide letter he'd previously typed on another Remington, dropping it on the desk to complete the deception. He then departed, needing only the discovery of the body of the young man and the cooperation of the police to complete the plan. Once the police declared the young Costes a suicide and a murderer, their investigation would cease and he would be shielded forever from the threat of justice."

A chastened and crestfallen Cullen crushed his cigar into the tumbler. "And he would have succeeded," he said in a low voice, "if not for you, Mr. Hawkes."

"I suggest you find that other Remington typewriter, Cullen. With it, you may be able to pin this on our man, assuming it remains in his possession, of course." Hawkes leaned back in his chair, frowning, and sank into deep thought for a few moments.

"Mr. Hawkes, do you know who the man is who is in back of all this?" broke in Cullen. "You give me the impression that you do."

"Come, at this point it is obvious. It is George Hammond behind it all. It can be no one else."

"Hammond!"

"The killing of his wife was no accident. It was she who was his target from the beginning. The attacks upon Dunmore served as subterfuge, a deceit to misdirect the course of the police investigation, to have you searching for a foeman who would want to see Franklin Dunmore dead, rather than for an enemy of Amelia Hammond."

For the second time within the last few minutes, Detective Cullen's mouth dropped open in absolute surprise and his gaze transformed to a look of absolute perplexity. "Hammond?" he managed to murmur at last. "Mr. Hawkes, My head spins."

"I'm sure it does, I must confess that I have some advantage over you regarding full knowledge of this case. I have been involved since the first attack upon Dunmore. He only told you—the police—of those attacks after Amelia Hammond was killed. I also have the advantage of my investigation of the grounds of Black Oak. I was there and back for a second time just today. I was certain it was Hammond before you knocked upon my door at the Dead Rabbits. Your announcement to me then, stating it was Robert Costes behind these murders, dumbfounded me at

118

that moment at least as much as my words have now startled you."

"Hammond. What makes you point the finger at him?"

Hawkes formed a triangle with the fingers of his hand and began to speak in the didactic fashion he so often was forced to utilize with me, that is, in the manner of a professor speaking to a rather slow student.

"I was suspicious from the first that the attacks upon Dunmore were not true attempts upon his life. In the first case he was at the complete mercy of the assailant, the garrote was about his neck and he was incapable of fending the attacker off, yet for no apparent reason he was released from that certain death. In the second case a shot was fired through his window, yet it was so wide of the mark, and he such a clear target, that either the shooter had to be completely inept regarding the use of firearms or had deliberately fired to miss. Since I had knowledge of the first attack against Dunmore, it was clear that the overshoot was deliberate."

"So someone was toying with him," broke in Cullen. "Wanted to frighten the man before finally finishing him off."

"That of course was a possibility. But there existed also the potentiality that the intent was not to kill at all but rather to create the appearance of wanting to kill. Why? I explored a couple of avenues but they led me nowhere. One possibility was that the purpose of the attacks was to unnerve Dunmore to the point where he could not function properly. I have the experience of a similar case years ago in which a man was about to negotiate a major business contract and his adversary thought it would benefit him if his rival's thinking was clouded. Yet that was not the case with Dunmore who is a quiet man with no real business interests. My investigation was at a standstill without more data. Unfortunately, that essential new information only came my way through the murder of Amelia Hammond.

"As I said, I already suspected that the attempts against Franklin Dunmore's life were false. And now another attempt had occurred. Was this a true attempt to end Dunmore's life?

119

One which hit an innocent? Was our man tired of his cat-and-mouse game? Or was this another try to simply frighten Dunmore, one which went terribly awry and resulted in the accidental death of an innocent victim? Or was it something else? I immediately added to my list of possibilities the thought that Mrs. Hammond was the intended victim all along and that the attacks against Dunmore were meant to disguise that. My trip to Black Oak and my investigation there served to enhance that consideration rather than dispel it.

"Since you have never been to Hammond's country home let me briefly describe the garden grounds and the rear of the house to you. The garden is accessible from the house only through the French Doors of the dining room. From the outside the garden is encircled by a tall brick wall broken by an old gate which opens upon a dirt road that passes by the back. Its rusted shut. Since the shot that killed Mrs. Hammond came from the garden, the police jumped to the conclusion that the shooter entered the grounds over this gate, fired his errant shot and left the same way. This conclusion appeared to be an obvious one under the circumstances–a stranger stalking Dunmore and following him to Black Oak from the city *would* have jumped over the gate–and the police accepted it without question.

"To my surprise, when I examined the grounds, I saw that, while the garden gate was rusted shut and had not been opened, no one had jumped over it. If the shooter entered and left this way, he had to jump over the closed gate. The ground was soft and anyone of the size and weight of our shooter hopping the gate would have left deep impressions in the ground. Yet there were no such impressions. There was only one explanation for this, that is, that the killer did not enter nor leave via the gate at all, but rather gained access to the garden another way. I searched for and subsequently found another door, hidden behind some thick hedges that permitted entry. Another way in and out of the garden.

"That door was a substantial discovery. If a killer had followed Dunmore from the city, it is highly unlikely that he would have chanced upon the door to use it. It was too well concealed by the hedges growing on both sides of the garden wall. I discovered it only because I searched for it. There remained only one possibility. The killer was someone very familiar with the garden grounds. Someone who was aware of the door's existence beforehand. Still, even being aware of the existence of this door, why use it? Why not hop over the gate regardless? The answer to this question was immediately obvious. The door was used for its convenience to the side entrance to the house. Our killer was someone in the house.

"Who? Obviously, only those not present in the dining room at the time of the shooting. That included the servants, Robert Costes, Doctor Rogers and George Hammond himself. I had previously determined that the attacker was in good trim and approximately five-foot-ten in height. Unfortunately all of these men fit that rather vague description. Of the suspects, I was inclined initially to lean away from Costes as he was the least familiar with the house. It was his first visit there. How could he know of the existence of the hidden door? However, he did later mention to me that he liked to read in the garden and spent much of his time there. it was possible that he explored the grounds and stumbled upon the door. My primary suspects then were Braxton, the newest employee of Hammond's, the good doctor, Robert Costes and lastly, George Hammond himself. William Huxley, the Hammond manservant, was too old and too short for consideration. You will recall that I asked you to look into the histories of these men, in particular searching for past injuries inflicted upon them by either Dunmore or George or Amelia Hammond. I was principally interested in learning whether any of them had past associations with either George or Amelia Hammond and had any reason, real or imagined, to seek revenge against them."

Cullen shook his head. "Couldn't find anything of interest. They were all straight arrows, never in trouble with the law. Even Braxton. And none of them had any quarrel with either Dunmore or the Hammonds."

"Which is also suggestive. I was leaning primarily towards George Hammond in any case. He did after all invite Dunmore to his home, rather strongly insisted upon doing so, and I had previous hints of his having economic problems, perhaps even marital problems. In that, I reasoned, might reside a motive to kill his wife."

"What? What are you talking about? Everyone said they were happily married and money is not a problem for the Hammonds."

Hawkes smiled. "There was an instance some time ago in which Hammond approached me in the Dead Rabbits, seeking a little company and conversation. It was a particularly wet night, with the rain coming down quite heavily. George Hammond is a man who takes care of himself, who believes in luxury, yet when I saw him that night his fine boots and pants were quite soiled and wet from the rain. It was clear he had walked the distance from his home to the Dead Rabbits rather than taking a carriage. Why? Was a cab unavailable? I asked if his own carriage was broken down and he replied it was in fine shape.

"It wasn't used by his wife as she had remained home by his own account. Even if his own carriage was not available to him, there's no shortage of cabs in this city. A man of Hammond's status would have had a servant seek one out for him. So, why should such a man walk on such a night? That query was actually two questions. One, the family carriage was not available to him for some reason that had nothing to do with its being broken down, what could that reason be? Also, Hammond did not then choose to hire a carriage to keep him dry. Again why? Could the answer be that he simply didn't have the fare?"

"Hammond not having money for a carriage? He has good and plenty it seems to me."

"Yes, it seemed so to me at the time also. His clothes were new and first-rate that night. And if I had any doubts about his financial wealth they were dispelled by his later extending invitations to friends and acquaintances to enjoy a few weeks in the country. That would be an expensive indulgence for a couple experiencing monetary problems. No, there was money in the Hammond home, yet, that night, Hammond walked in the rain to the Society. Why? If money was not a problem otherwise, and should not have been a problem regarding his obtaining a cab, then what could explain this apparent anomaly in behavior on his part? A peculiar little problem. A little out of the common. One which piqued my curiosity as I looked at him."

"I'm sure I have no idea as to the answer."

"As I said, there were two questions to be answered. First, why wasn't his own carriage available to him? That question we will leave aside for now. Second, even if the carriage is not available, why not summon and pay for another? As I said, a possible answer to the second question was that he could spare no funds to pay for one. A bit of a conjecture, I admit, but also a very likely one. Taking this as our hypotheses the question becomes: Why wouldn't a man such as this have the fare for a cab ride? To understand this, we must investigate the source of his money. Again an answer presents itself. His income from his legal firm was not as it should be and he had no access to funds from that direction. We can thus infer that his business is doing poorly. Yet, was that his only source of capital? Of course not, he was married into a family of wealth and so was not without access to money from that direction. His wife is very rich, to put it quite bluntly. Now, if his business is doing poorly then it must follow that he was financially dependent upon obtaining funds from his wife. Having lost his own income, he must, and quite naturally would, look to her for money. Could the wife's family riches also be depleted? A possibility but a doubtful one. The expensive new clothes suggested opulence instead. So we assume Amelia Hammond has money. Again we ask, why didn't he take a cab that rainy night? If short of funds himself, he had to only ask his wife for the necessary money. Why would a loving wife refuse such a small request? Here again, a possible answer presented itself. Hammond had at some time, perhaps that very night, fought with his wife and she, in her anger, denied him the funds he needed. Here was a man, I thought then, who was at the

123

mercy of his wife's good will. This conclusion was a bit of a reach, I admit, yet it did explain the facts. It also answered the question as to why Hammond didn't ride in the family carriage that night. His wife forbid him to use it. I concluded that night that Mr. George Hammond was a man very much under the thumb of his wife. I could not be certain of this of course. It was speculation as much as reasoning, but it was speculation I retained in the back of my mind when I first traveled to Black Oak."

Cullen gazed in wonder. "Mr. Hawkes, you are a marvel. You see puzzles and solutions where others see rain and muddy boots. Why, if we had a few men like you on the New York City force, I'm certain there'd be an end to crime in a short time."

Hawkes, a man always susceptible to compliments regarding his unique skills, smiled his appreciation of the compliment just prior to his waving it away. "Elementary sir." Here the smile slipped away. "But you compliment me too quickly. I must hasten to add that I have been very remiss in this matter. It is as much through my own incompetence, as through the desire of the killer, that Franklin Dunmore and Robert Costes have lost their lives. If I had been sharper, I might very well have had Hammond in handcuffs the first time I went to Black Oak. I'd have stopped him then and there and his next two killings would never have taken place. I was slow, very slow in this case."

"How so?" asked Cullen.

"When I first went to Black Oak and examined the garden grounds, I noted the presence of a sundial in the centre of the grounds. It was brand-new. I learned that it was a birthday present from Hammond to his wife who was very fond of working in the garden."

"What does a sundial have to do with anything?"

"The thought came to me yesterday. A careful man, plotting such a murder as this, might have planned to dispose of the weapon he used as soon as possible. The path through the garden door and along the house to the side entrance is not normally used and the odds favored the killer that he would not accidentally run into anyone as he returned to the house. But what if he did and still carried his Smith & Wesson? It would prove to be embarrassing."

"To say the least," replied Cullen.

"Yes, his guilt would be evident on the spot. But without the weapon in his possession, he could always attempt to explain his presence there. So the question became: Where would a killer, seeking to hide his weapon as quickly as possible, conceal the Smith & Wesson? Nothing could be more expeditious than hiding it right in the garden immediately after the shooting. The newest addition to the garden, purchased by the man I suspected in the killing, was the sundial. Was it possible that it was purchased to serve as more than a decoration? I returned to Black Oak and went to it. Lifting it, I found a hollowed out cavity dug out of the earth beneath. It was empty by then but it was the right size to conceal the pistol and stock. I knew at once that I had found the hiding place for the murder weapon. It had since been moved of course. The sundial had been purchased for no other reason than to provide a hiding place for the Smith & Wesson. I have no doubt that if I had made this discovery upon my first investigation, as I should have done, the pistol would have still been there to greet my eyes. I could have had Hammond arrested for the murder of his wife that very day and Dunmore and Costes would still be alive."

"I don't understand. Why kill Dunmore at all if it was his wife he wanted dead? He already had that."

"That is obvious. He now must kill Dunmore. To suddenly cease in the attacks against the man might reveal that Amelia Hammond was the intended victim all along. It would go against the whole intent of his plan. I warned Dunmore to get a bodyguard for himself knowing the attacks would have to continue. At that time, although I suspected Hammond, I could not accuse him. Not without absolute proof of his guilt. To make such an accusation against the man would have created a scandal. The accusation would have damaged his reputation even if later I'd been proven wrong. But I could stress the danger to

Dunmore which I did. He at last obtained a bodyguard as I had suggested from the outset. Unfortunately the protection was not sufficient to keep him alive."

"I wouldn't be too hard on myself, Mr. Hawkes. The way you've seen to the bottom of all this is, to say the least, quite extraordinary. If you took one wrong step along the way, it is quite different from the wrong road the police have walked. That includes me. I fell for it all hook, line and sinker. I spoke to Hammond and he struck me as nothing less than a grieving husband devastated by the loss of his wife."

"Yes, he is quite the consummate actor," returned Hawkes. "And startlingly clever. He hammered out this scheme right down to the smallest detail. I would not be surprised to learn, for example, that the sole reason for his inviting Doctor Rogers up to Black Oak along with his other guests was to have a physician on hand to prescribe a sedative to him and keep the police from interviewing him immediately after the murder."

"You say we can nail him if we find the other typewriter?" said Cullen. "You're certain you can tell which typewriter that suicide note was written on?"

"Certainly. As far as I can see, obtaining that second Remington in his possession is your only hope. Everything I've told you does not constitute hard evidence. I suggest you make an immediate search of Hammond's home and office. With luck you'll find the Remington and you'll have him. Without it—" Hawkes shook his head. "I fear he may yet escape justice."

"I'll get some men right now," stated Cullen, standing, his face set like stone. "You'll come with us?"

"Of course," replied Hawkes, pushing himself up from the table. "I would not miss the pleasure of seeing handcuffs clapped upon the wrists of Mr. George Hammond for all the world."

That pleasure which Simon Hawkes was so keenly anticipating was not to be achieved. A thorough search of the premises of George Hammond's home and office failed to locate the particular Remington typewriter which would confirm the murderer's guilt, seal his fate and send him to the newly instituted means of execution in the State of New York, the electrical chair. Both Cullen and Hawkes had to endure Hammond's smug sense of certitude in his own cleverness and an expression akin to an audacious sneer of contempt for the detectives as he watched them leave his home empty-handed.

A trip to Black Oak and a search of that home and the surrounding lands and property also failed to locate the Remington. Despite Simon Hawkes ferreting out the truth behind the astoundingly wicked plot of murder assembled by George Hammond against his wife, the man he knew to be guilty of three heinous murders remained beyond the reach and punishment of the legal authorities and justice.

CHAPTER NINETEEN

"**M**r. Hawkes, a pleasure to see you again." George Hammond forced a smile onto his face as his sarcastic words greeted Simon Hawkes. He was seated in a chair by the fire in the main room of the Dead Rabbits, a glass of fine cognac in hand, the picture of contentment and prosperity. He was a man at peace with the world.

"Mr. Hammond, do you mind if I join you by the fire?" asked Hawkes. "I'd like a few words with you."

"Now, there won't be a scene, will there, Simon?"

"Doubtful," replied Hawkes, placing himself in the armchair opposite Hammond.

"You've already caused some damage to my reputation," complained Hammond. "Why there are some who actually believe I could be responsible for my wonderful Amelia's death, thanks to you."

"You know of your own guilt," remarked Hawkes. "Any damage to your reputation is of your own doing. If I had my way, and if justice was perfect in this imperfect world, you would be more concerned now with your coming execution then with the opinion of others."

"What do you want, Simon?" Hammond's tone turned angry. "Please say it and then be on your way."

"I came to ask you what you did with the typewriting machine upon which you typed Costes supposed suicide note," responded Hawkes matter-of-factly. "Also, I wonder how you knew it was necessary to dispose of it. It surprises me that you knew enough to do that. Most would not."

Hammond first gazed at Hawkes in astonishment, then the insufferable smirk of superiority he had displayed previously, on the day Cullen and Hawkes and a few uniformed police had searched his home for the Remington, appeared once again upon his face. "Do you think me a fool, Simon? What is it? Do you have someone in earshot waiting for me to blurt my guilt? I wouldn't expect anything so clumsy from you." He looked about and saw no one in close proximity. Still he continued his ruse. "You know I had nothing to do with my wife's murder, despite your fanciful tale to the contrary. Why, I'd have to be inordinately clever to come up with a scheme such as you credit to me, wouldn't I?" The last sentence was a gloat of superiority on Hammond's part and he placed a grin upon the end of it just prior to taking another sip of cognac from the snifter in his hand.

"Clever yes, but not inordinately so. If I hadn't been off my game, I would have had you right off," responded Hawkes. "You were as much lucky as clever."

"Was I?"

"Yes, I should have discovered your little hiding place for your Smith & Wesson the first day I was at Black Oak. The little hollow you dug out beneath the sundial. I have no doubt that if I had looked under it that day I would have found the murder weapon lying there. Its presence would have pointed the finger of probable guilt towards you, as it was you who made the purchase of the sundial. It certainly would have allowed me to accuse you right then and there."

Hammond blinked in surprise. "The sundial–" he murmured. "How, how could you possibly know the gun was hidden under it?"

"Perhaps if you answer my questions, I would be inclined to answer yours."

Hammond chuckled. "I repeat I did not kill my wife. That's the truth of it. However, if I had, which I did not, and if that suicide note of Costes was false and I had typed it, which I did not, then I indeed would have gotten rid of the typewriter. I had read an account recently in an old copy of a weekly news journal, of a crime solved by Scotland Yard in your home country. They were able to differentiate between two separate machines which in all regards appeared identical. This was due to the way the typewritten letters appeared on the paper. I was quite astounded and I thought to myself, if I ever commit a crime in which a typewriter is used, which of course I never would, then I would have to be certain to dispose of it as soon as possible." His gaze was more haughty, more insufferable, than ever.

"Why not type the note on Costes' typewriting machine?"

"Speaking hypothetically, I would say, if someone killed Costes, that someone may not be too familiar with using the machines and most likely would not want to spend a few hours typing, perhaps until dawn, in the dead man's apartment trying to write the lengthy explanation that was found. Better to type it beforehand. One does what one can and then hopes for the best at times. I daresay most detectives would have accepted the note as typewritten by Costes without question. You seem to be the exception to the rule, Simon. Personally, I still believe it was written by Costes, despite your claim to the contrary. Perhaps he wrote it on another Remington? Isn't that possible? You really have spun a hurtful tale, hurtful to me, with your spurious little theory."

"Why not type the note before giving the machine to him?"

"You still suggest I had something to do with this? And I must still insist I did not. However, I did say the article about typewriting machines appeared recently didn't I? *After* Costes was in possession of the machine? A stroke of good luck for certain, if I was the killer. In fact the article appeared only a day or so before Costes was found dead." A smile appeared on Hammond's lips. "Good fortune comes to those who most deserve it."

"You are proud of what you've done, aren't you? There's not an ounce of remorse within you for the many lives you've taken."

"Again I repeat, I've done nothing. But if I had, what purpose would be served by remorse? Lives are lost every day. We will all die sooner or later. So three people had their deaths hastened a bit? So what? One hundred years from now they would have been dead in any case. Simon, wake up and look about you. Don't you see the revolution taking place? Science is proving all the old myths are just that–old myths. There's no such thing as morality. And remorse is for fools. There is only force. Cause and effect. We are either moved by other forces or we are a force to move others. There is no God, Simon, except in our collective minds. By simply exorcising Him, some may be able to gain a new freedom, isn't that so? Each individual now holds the power to be his own god. Are you capable of seeing that?"

Hawkes gazed at the cocksure man, certain he was looking at nothing less than a physical manifestation of absolute evil. His distaste was evident in his expression and Hammond saw it, frowning in response even while his eyes twinkled with pleasure. "I see, Simon, that you are not convinced," he said simply. "Pity. You ask for honesty so I'll give you some. Although I didn't kill Amelia I do confess to a certain amount of contentment that someone else did."

"Your marriage was less than perfect," replied Simon, "and she held the purse strings, much to your chagrin."

Again, Hammond's eyes widened in surprise. "Why, you do continue to amaze me. How on earth could you know that? No one does. Not even our, ah, *my* servants. Still my pleasure over Amelia's demise is not just with regard to the money I have so happily inherited. I'm in love, Simon, passionately so, and Amelia's death frees me from the pretense of loving her while in fact loving another."

Hawkes grunted, surprised by the admission.

"I never really loved Amelia," continued Hammond. "Oh, she was nice enough but there was no passion there for me. I married her for her name and her money. I didn't think I was capable of that all-consuming love the poets write of. And then, a year ago, I met someone. She's beautiful. Oh, I've had affairs with beautiful women before, but this was different. The others– I've always felt outside of the affair somehow. But this–and this was a shock to me–I was for the first time in my life totally and passionately in love. For the first time in my life I experienced the true power of that emotion. The very sight, no, the thought of her, filled me with desire. To hold her was, and is, an overwhelming delight, a delicious pleasure." He took another sip of cognac and added in a low tone filled with humour. "Why, I do believe I would kill for her–if I ever had to."

"How did Robert Costes become involved in your plans?"

"Plans? What plans? You keep talking as if I've done something. Very annoying, Simon, I must say. If you're asking how Robert came to work for my firm, it's quite simple. My firm was looking for good men to bring into it. Good men are hard to find and the best resource is often to raid the personnel of another establishment. Of course, before hiring anyone, a complete investigation is made of their background. That is standard procedure in my firm. Costes was one of those investigated. His change of name was discovered. His real name was Costispoti. The same last name as one of my liaisons, Angela Costispoti. Imagine my surprise to discover that the very pretty little trollop I was being pleasured by was Mr. Costes' own sister. What's more, again to my surprise, she had once worked for Franklin Dunmore as a housemaid. I knew I had to hire a young man of such unique–skills–as those possessed by Robert Costes immediately. With my hiring of him things very soon–came together quite well. Between you and me, Simon, I do confess to being the one who got the very alluring Angela Costispoti pregnant. Poor Robert was incorrect in his belief that it was Franklin Dunmore as he wrote in his suicide note. Perhaps if he knew the truth he would have killed me instead of Frank. I promised her marriage you see, after which she very rashly threw all caution to the winds on my behalf. Once she was pregnant, I of course told her marriage was out of the question. She was a fool to have thought it possible. I was quite cruel in the way I dismissed her I must admit, but there's no law against treating whores badly, is there Simon?"

"You continue to astound me, sir," said an incredulous Simon Hawkes.

In response, Hammond simply shrugged his shoulders and smiled once again. Then, leaning closer to Hawkes and speaking in a barely perceptible whisper: "At Black Oak, when you saw me, I'd been up all night–I'd taken amphetamine–have you heard of it?–a remarkable new stimulant–to keep me awake–and not the laudanum the doctor prescribed. It made me a rather miserable looking thing, did it not? After being awake all night, I looked like a suffering husband, didn't I?"

Sherlock Holmes had met many a criminal in his day but, in recounting this singular history to me, he found it necessary to then halt in the narrative to state that he was of the personal opinion that he had never before come into contact with a man who so filled him with revulsion or who so appeared to be the embodiment of amorality and evil as did George Hammond at that moment. Even the baneful corruption that radiated from the snarling, puckered eyes of Professor Moriarty himself appeared to be incapable of matching the total absence of anything good that constituted the soul of George Hammond.

George Hammond, seeing the expression of loathing on Hawkes' face laughed heartily and gulped down the last of the cognac. "Remember that night we first talked, the fight between Charlie and Frank? I thought then that even the fates were on my side. Anything after that was meant to be. And I was right, wasn't I? There you have it, Simon. As I said, I'm innocent as a new-born babe. Now if you will excuse me, since you seem to have no intention of leaving and I've grown weary of your company, I will be off. In the future, sir, please keep your distance from me. Good day."

Hawkes watched the back of the man as he strode out of the room and then turned to look into the fire, fixing his gaze upon the flickering flames in front of him. He remained silent and still for a time and then, with the gesture of a man finally taking a decision he'd long debated and even agonized over, he rose to his feet and, following the same path George Hammond had taken minutes ago, walked out of the room.

133

CHAPTER TWENTY

At quarter past the noon hour the next day found Simon sitting in a small Italian eatery located on Hester Street. Diagonally across the street from the eatery was the little butcher shop through which the Costispoti family earned their living. Simon, having come an hour earlier and having his choice of seats, was at the table nearest the window which afforded him a wide view of the street. Slowly, as the lunch hour had approached, the place had filled up around him and now the room was filled with the buzz of conversation and the sounds of hungry people devouring their meals. The door to the eatery was opened to permit entry of cooling air off the street and so relieve the stuffy atmosphere within the cramped room.

Across the street, three young girls looking to be nine or ten years of age were jumping rope and calling out a sing-song of a child's poem. Now and then, the sound of their singing and that of their laughter rose above the cacophony of other noise surrounding Hawkes. They were playing directly in front of the Costispoti butcher shop and, behind the children and in back of the glass of the shop window, Hawkes caught the gleaming glint of light sparkling off the blade of a large cleaver. The butcher, one of Roberto Costispoti's brothers, was cutting fresh meat on a chopping block, preparing it for sale.

The cleaver moved up and down, catching and losing the sunlight in a rhythm which matched that of the spinning rope and the skip of the young girl now in the middle, between her two friends. Simon pondered the juxtaposition of the two events–wasn't much of human life contained in the picture now being presented to him?–the butcher cutting his slaughtered meat and the singing of the young children–the brutality of the necessity of life behind the apparent innocence of it.

Simon finished up the last remnants of the small meal he'd ordered–he'd eaten his lunch slowly–and now, finishing his

134

food, he paid his bill and left the crowded eatery, walking across the street towards the butcher shop sitting behind the laughing children at play.

CHAPTER TWENTY-ONE

It was a windy, blustery night, cold, the air containing more than a hint of the coming winter. In the black chill of the night, huddled deep in the shadows that fell about the sidewalk in front of the Hammond home, was a shadow deeper than the surrounding shadows. A form so indistinct that even if one were looking for it, it was possible to let one's sight slide right past it without picking it out of the surrounding darkness.

Directly in front of the house, at the kerb, sat the Hammond carriage, waiting for George Hammond to appear. Hammond's driver however was not the man who sat in the chill with the reins in his hands. This was another man, a little shorter and wider than the true driver who was now bound and gagged and lying unconscious behind a hedge off to the side of the house. The variance in the size and shape of the man replacing the coachman would not be noticed, clad as he was in the driver's hat and coat. What parts of him were not disguised by the clothes he wore would be hidden by the night. In the dark he was little more than a hunched silhouette sitting in blackness.

Inside the house, George Hammond sat in his favourite chair, puffing contentedly on an expensive cigar. Amelia had never allowed him to smoke in the house. The new woman of the house, his mistress, was not so demanding. Poor Amelia, she didn't know she was her own worst enemy. She had made her own killing a necessity. It was, he told himself with some pride, an act of courage.

Through her murder he had achieved a kind of nobility for he was a man who *dared*, a man not bound by the restrictions of others. He drew on the cigar and released the smoke, watching the white cloud as it floated softly in front of his eyes, its swirls and movements performing for him. His thoughts and emotions were dominated by the joy, the rush of exultation, of appreciation of his own courage in choosing to create his own

136

destiny. He had risked all to do it, and had won. He chuckled now, recalling his own nervousness at the start of it. He dared to kill and was, at first, awed by his own audacity.

Hawkes had shocked him, the way he had seen through the mystery, seen through the cleverness of his plan and got to the truth. But even that proved relatively harmless in the end for there was no evidence against him. Nothing more than surmise and conjecture. Even the truth could not injure him. A little hurt to his reputation perhaps, but it was money and not reputation that most people responded to, and he had plenty of money now.

Hammond glanced about the room. The furniture, selected by his wife, was not to his taste. It would have to be sold and new pieces purchased.

The mantle clock struck the hour. It was time to leave. A night in the Tenderloin district, and the pleasures he would find there, awaited him. He crushed out the cigar, now reduced to ashes and a chewed stump, in the ashtray and pushed himself out of the chair. The hour was getting late but the night, for him at least, was just beginning. He was a man who believed the best pleasures of life could be purchased when the sun set at the end of the day.

Exiting his home, his face wearing a boyish enthusiasm, he drew his frock-coat closer around him, feeling the night's chill. Going to his carriage, he barked his destination with barely a glance to the silhouetted driver and climbed inside. The windows were drawn up on both sides as he preferred, keeping prying eyes from entering the interior of the carriage. As the carriage pulled away, it swayed as though a wheel had hit a small depression in the road. Hammond cursed the carelessness of his driver, unaware of the true cause of the carriage's swaying–the man who was in hiding had jumped upon the rear of the carriage and was now holding on, a secret rider in the night.

It was not the gas-lit streets of the Tenderloin district that greeted Hammond when the carriage came to a stop and he opened the door to depart, but rather the desolation and near total darkness of what seemed at first to be open countryside.

Following a few moments in which his eyes could better discern the surrounding area, he saw that he was in the midst of a graveyard. A hazy gauze of mist curled about the wheels of the carriage and floated about his feet as though seeking to attach itself to him. His eyes, filled with an angry questioning, went up to complain to the dark form of the driver but the coachman was already gone from his seat. His absence halted Hammond's complaint before he could give voice to it. What was happening here?

He turned back to gaze into the darkness in front of him as he heard his own name being muttered, spoken like a denunciation. A lantern's light was suddenly uncovered and gleamed at him, blinding him for the instant and he raised his arm to cover his eyes from it.

"Who are you?" demanded Hammond. "Why am I here?" His only answer for the moment was the moan of the branches of the trees overhead, moving in the wind. Suddenly the darkness here seemed somehow deeper, more palpable, another separate presence in the night.

Another silhouette moved in front of him, to his left, and entered into the light. Was it his imagination or did that face remind him of someone, someone he had once known? The man still wore his coachman's coat, the hat had been discarded. A revolver, held in the man's hand, was pointed towards Hammond's chest and Hammond's now fear-filled eyes went to it.

"What are you? Thieves?" There was more fright than protest in Hammond's voice now.

Another man came into the lantern's light, older, his face a mask of rage and loathing. In his hand, to Hammond's horror, was not another pistol but a long-bladed butcher's knife. Around him, the wind swirled, the branches continued to moan, and from somewhere within their dark canopy overhead there came to his ears the high-pitched screech of an owl. It might have been the sound of his own heart screaming its fear to him. His hand went to the pocket of his coat, reaching for the pistol it contained but it never reached it as the blade of the knife came up towards him, so swiftly! and sweep across his constricted throat.

The lantern's eye stared down upon Hammond's lifeless body lying on the ground at the feet of the men, and gazed for a few seconds at the murderer before its beam was turned away. Then the three men walked off slowly into the darkness, their sounds of movement and muttered words of satisfaction unheard by the souls of the dead surrounding them.

CHAPTER TWENTY-TWO

"**I** read of Hammond's murder in the Times the following day," said Holmes as, after relating to me the very grim conclusion of his history of murder in New York City, he rose from his chair and strode over to his pouch of tobacco to refill his pipe. He then motioned to the spirit case and gasogene. "I cannot say it caused me any distress," he added as he returned to his chair after I declined his offer of a drink. We were seated in the parlor of his home outside London, from which, now, he seldom strayed.

"You told the Costispoti family of Hammond's crimes," I told him, "You knew they would kill him."

"I confess that the thought had occurred to me." stated Holmes in a matter-of-fact manner that chilled me. "However, I must tell you that the New York police investigated that possibility and found no evidence against Roberto Costispoti's father and brothers. Surely, if such expertise could be brought to bear against them, and if they were indeed guilty, they would have been found out," he added, his voice heavy with sarcasm. Then, in response to the expression of dismay that no doubt sat upon my features, he said, "It is perhaps lamentable that we must at times search for justice outside those institutions we create to supply it. I can assure you, Watson, I gave very sincere thought to the possible consequences which might occur once I related Hammond's crimes to Mr. Costispoti. Although the New York police apparently proved otherwise, I like to believe that the man did not disappoint me. It is perhaps ironic that I was depending upon the exercise of the man's sense of honour, the same sense of honour I condemned when it was directed against his poor daughter at her time of severe need."

"Holmes, you are in part responsible for a man's death!"

"The alternative was to allow a murderer, a triple murderer, to go unpunished." A cloud of smoke rose from his pipe to the ceiling, for the moment obscuring his face. "I believe I took the proper action, and I have no less belief that, if indeed it was an act of revenge on the part of the Costispoti family that eliminated Mr. Hammond's connection to this world, Mr. Costispoti took the proper action as well. Would it have been preferable to do nothing and so let the man escape punishment for his crimes?"

I had to admit that I did not think so.

"You see, my dear Watson," he added after a few seconds of silence between us, "it is justice itself which is paramount, not our laws and institutions which only maintain validity while they are capable of properly serving it. In this case the sole hope for the attainment of justice was left to me–and the Costispoti family which had been so monstrously harmed. Remember, Watson, Mr. George Hammond was responsible not only directly for Robert Costispoti's death but indirectly for Angela Costispoti's as well. I tell you, Watson, I have never seen a man, neither before nor after, who was so profoundly and deeply evil as was the American, George Hammond."

"The police never connected Hammond's killing with the Costispoti family?" I asked. "Somehow I find that quite incredible. Who else would have done such a thing?"

"The police attributed it to robbers, although Hammond's wallet and gold pocket watch remained upon him. They decided that Hammond resisted the thieves and they ran off, horrified by what they had done, after killing him. Faulty reasoning there, I would imagine. I was asked to look into the matter but I declined, feigning the necessity of another obligation. I had no desire to find Hammond's true killers."

"It-It seems wrong somehow," I murmured.

Holmes smiled at me through another cloud of smoke. "Now, Watson, I seem to recall the fine words of praise you offered me in that short and erroneous narrative you entitled "The Adventure of the Final Problem". I believe you then regarded me as 'the best and wisest man' you had ever known. I know it is a bit unfair of me to quote you now as you thought those words to be my final eulogy at the time, but nevertheless I remind you of them and I use them now to end this discussion of morality. It is after all, to some degree at least, an ever-changing philosophy. Morality I mean. Perhaps some day, science will reduce it to immutable fact but that future escapes us now. For now we can turn our attention to more pleasant things. I have a fine cook who is just short of the wonderful fare formerly provided us by our dear Mrs. Hudson, who is sorely missed. I tell by the sounds and odors coming to me that dinner is just a quarter-hour or so away. I trust you will stay and join me? I have taken up all our time with an old history from years ago. Perhaps you can supply me with more up-to-date information regarding the streets of London."